"Your Mouth Is Open, Mrs. Delaney."

He lowered his v___ ___easingly. "I appreciate it."

Lindsey'___ ___ of outrage was muffled by
t___ ___ hard mouth on hers. He
___ astonishment to invade
___ er mouth with his
___ devastatingly thorough
___ ___eavor designed to leave her
___ ___g. She was aware of Marcus Stafford with
___ ery muscle, nerve and bone in her body—aware
of the denim-clad thighs brushing against her bare
legs, aware of the massive muscles of his chest
which burned her through the thin material of her
tank top and aware of his plundering, hard mouth
that intrigued her vulnerable lips. When she could
no longer hide her unwilling response to his kiss, he
lifted her feet off the ground, then set her down
away from him. "Having successfully gained your
interest, I'll get back to work."

JANET JOYCE

resides in Ohio, happily married to the man who
swept her off her feet as a college coed; she admits
that her own romance is what prompted her writing
career. She and her family like camping, traveling and
are avid fans of college football. She is an accomplished pianist, enjoys composing her own lyrics and
reads voraciously, especially the romances she loves.

Dear Reader:

Silhouette has always tried to give you exactly what you want. When you asked for increased realism, deeper characterization and greater length, we brought you Silhouette Special Editions. When you asked for increased sensuality, we brought you Silhouette Desire. Now you ask for books with the length and depth of Special Editions, the sensuality of Desire, but with something else besides, something that no one else offers. Now we bring you SILHOUETTE INTIMATE MOMENTS, true romance novels, longer than the usual, with all the depth that length requires. More sensuous than the usual, with characters whose maturity matches that sensuality. Books with the ingredient no one else has tapped: excitement.

There is an electricity between two people in love that makes everything they do magic, larger than life—and this is what we bring you in SILHOUETTE INTIMATE MOMENTS. Look for them wherever you buy books.

These books are for the woman who wants more than she has ever had before. These books are for you. As always, we look forward to your comments and suggestions. You can write to me at the address below:

Karen Solem
Editor-in-Chief
Silhouette Books
P.O. Box 769
New York, N.Y. 10019

JANET JOYCE
Man Of The House

Silhouette Desire

Published by Silhouette Books New York

America's Publisher of Contemporary Romance

Other Silhouette Books by Janet Joyce

Winter Lady

SILHOUETTE BOOKS, a Simon & Schuster Division of
GULF & WESTERN CORPORATION
1230 Avenue of the Americas, New York, N.Y. 10020

ISBN: 0-671-46409-4

First Silhouette Books printing June, 1983

10 9 8 7 6 5 4 3 2 1

America's Publisher of Contemporary Romance

Printed in the U.S.A.

Man Of The House

1

Lindsey pulled back the pink chintz curtains from the large bay window in her daughters' bedroom and watched below until Maggie Rollins emerged onto the cracked sidewalk in front of their house with her two boisterous young charges. The trio was on their way to the school playground. Lindsey's four-year-old twin girls, Kelly and Carrie, were tugging impatiently on the gray-haired woman's hands, anxious to reach the playground's big slide and towering swings. Lindsey slid the window open in order to call out one last motherly warning before letting the threesome march out of sight.

"Take care of Maggie, girls. I'm counting on you to look both ways when you help her cross the street." She waited until she saw the amused smile widen across Maggie's lined cheeks as the two little girls immediately became more solicitous, grasping the hands of their slow-moving friend and kindly escorting her across the tree-lined street. Lindsey captured two blow-away kisses in her hands and waved to her daughters, then sighed with relief when they finally rounded the corner and walked out of sight.

She took a deep breath of the fragrant June air. Poppies were blossoming red in the garden, surrounded by white bridal wreath. Along the front walk perfumed pink and white peonies were in full bloom. The large oak tree that shaded the front yard with a trellis of leaves was filled with songbirds greeting the sun. Lindsey planned to cut some fresh flowers for Elizabeth, as soon as she got a spare minute, and place them in her room. Maybe that would bring pleasure to a face that had not smiled since she moved into the big old Victorian house, three weeks ago.

Lindsey understood Elizabeth's sadness and hoped that she and her family could help the woman remove the shroud of loneliness that surrounded her. Elizabeth Milford had lost her husband of forty years last summer, while Lindsey Delaney had been a widow for three years. There was a vast difference in their ages and in their situations, but even at twenty-seven, with two four-year-olds to keep her busy, Lindsey still felt the void of losing her life's partner.

She realized that Peter had not always been the ideal husband, yet she missed the secure feeling she had once enjoyed as his wife. His work had kept him away from their home for long periods, but even so, Lindsey had felt anchored in a safe mooring. His death had cast her adrift and demonstrated to her that she had never really been on course in the first place. Never again would she allow herself to become so dependent on another person that she could not weather by herself the inevitable storms that life held.

No, she would not allow herself to become as helplessly dependent as Elizabeth had, with every facet of her life revolving around her mate. Unable to bear living in her home of nearly forty years, Elizabeth had sold it; under the persuasion of her grown children, she had moved into a small cottage in a retirement village. But she had not been happy there. Lindsey hoped that her large house would provide the atmosphere of tradition and stability that Elizabeth needed.

She glanced around her at the carved woodwork of her daughters' room, the same warm oak trim that graced every room, and smiled inwardly. It was a friendly house, meant to be filled with a family. A house that had weathered many years, sheltered many families and still stood straight and proud, a graceful example of architecture from another time. When this house had been new, the gazebo-style bandstand that still stood in the small town square had been in weekly use, providing entertainment during the long, lazy summers. It had been a time when families gathered every evening on wide front porches to "take the evening air," or strolled down the streets, stopping to chat with their neighbors along the way.

Lindsey remembered the day she and Peter had driven by the house. She had fallen in love with it, delighted to see the For Sale sign in the front yard. The gingerbread-trimmed white house represented everything Lindsey thought a family home should be. Having just discovered that she was carrying twins, she was determined that her children would be born to this house, and after much persuasion, Peter had agreed. He had argued that it would need constant repairs, but Lindsey had countered that they would be minor ones and that the house was structurally more sound than most new houses. He had grumbled and begrudgingly done the refurbishments that had been necessary immediately. In the years since his death, Lindsey had learned to cope with a multitude of minor fix-it jobs.

The thought of repairs brought her back to the present, and she watched hopefully as a large black car turned onto the street, then was disappointed when it didn't pull into the driveway. She had successfully gotten the twins off, and it was time to find out why her volunteer had not yet arrived to begin work on the roof—a job she was unable to tackle.

She crossed the hall, and walked into her room, looking for the hairbrush she needed. She found it atop her antique cherry dressing table and picked it up. Gathering her long sable hair into a ponytail, she took a quick glance in her mirror. She blinked her large brown eyes, but when they reopened, her image was still the same. How could a twenty-seven-year-old woman with two children look so immature? In cutoff shorts and a pink tank top, she looked like a teenager. She picked up a tube of coral lipstick and applied a light gloss to her childishly pink mouth, shrugging at the result. Maybe a haircut would make her look her age. She wrinkled her nose at the mirror, then turned and ran lightly out of her room and down the carpeted stairs.

Following her nose to the kitchen, she promised herself she would pose the polite question that needed to be asked *before* she devoured the delicacies she knew were waiting for her: "Are you certain your son doesn't mind coming to fix our roof?"

As she entered the large warm kitchen through the swinging wood door, Lindsey turned doubtful brown eyes on Vera Stafford. She smiled at both women who were busy at the long counter, wondering how long they had already been working this morning. But when she asked her question, Vera shook her head dismissively, the movement unable to jar even one silver strand loose from its tightly wound chignon.

"Nonsense! Marcus is more than happy to do it. He wants to repay your kindness to me. He's grateful that I've found such a nice home with you, since he travels so much. Baldridge is only twenty miles south of Columbus. Besides, it will do him good to get away from his work for the weekend." She picked up a large bowl of apples and carried them to the oak pedestal table in the center of the room.

Lindsey doubted that Vera's son would consider replacing several missing shingles in a steadily deteriorating roof as "getting away from work." She didn't want to insult Vera, but she suspected that her dear lodger had not informed the man that he would have to handle the job alone. There was no money to hire a roofer and neither Lindsey's grandmother Althea, Vera, Elizabeth nor Maggie was about to climb up on the roof. And though the twins would certainly be willing, they would be of no help. That left Lindsey herself, and she had an unsettling fear of high places.

When Vera had told her that her son—a geophysicist of all things—was willing to repair their leaky roof, Lindsey had agreed, but with a great deal of misgiving. From what she had heard about Marcus Stafford from his mother, he probably wouldn't recognize a hammer if he saw one. He evidently spent all his time preparing charts and maps that showed formations of underground mineral deposits. All the rock analysis in the world would not help reshingle Lindsey's roof. She needed a practical man who didn't mind physical labor, not a middle-aged bachelor who spent most of his time jetting around the world. At least the man seemed to know what materials were required for the job. He had conveyed through his mother a list of tools and supplies he needed, and they were neatly stacked in the screened-in front porch waiting for him.

"I hope he knows what he has let himself in for." Lindsey pulled out a chair and reached for a homemade cinnamon bun as she sat down. "I'm going to weigh a ton if I don't stop eating these things," she muttered as her teeth sank into the sweet confection, warm from the oven. She made a face at the petite, plump woman, enveloped in a blue gingham apron, who was removing another pan of fresh rolls from the ancient white Caloric stove. "Someday you'll have to show me how to make these, Grandma."

Althea Patterson beamed at Lindsey from across the room, her faded blue eyes brightening with pleasure. "We'll have you fattened up yet, Lindy. You've had far too much on your shoulders since Peter's death, and you're worn out. No matter what we do to help, it's nothing compared to what you do around here."

Lindsey made no comment, unable to hear mention of Peter's name without feeling guilt. He had died in a car accident three years ago, and she had yet to shed a single tear.

At first, she had been in a state of shock so great she had been unable to react. But afterwards, when the initial shock had worn off, resentment had taken its place. Peter, her workaholic husband, had left her alone to contend with a stack of unpaid debts, two very young children and a big old house in desperate need of repair. He had not even thought to protect her by keeping up the payments on his life insurance. Her salary as an elementary schoolteacher was not enough to keep up with all the expenses. Within three months of the accident, Lindsey had been on the verge of losing her house. That was when she had had the idea of taking in boarders.

Her grandmother had come to help Lindsey through the difficult days preceding the funeral and had stayed on to help with the twins. Althea had been alone in a rapidly decaying old neighborhood in Cleveland, and was happy to leave it for what had been initially planned as a visit of a few weeks. As the time passed, Lindsey realized how much she depended on her grandmother, the woman who had reared her after her parents' deaths. She asked Althea if she would be willing to join forces and help her with the twins, so she could keep her job and provide Althea with a home and family. Althea had loved the idea. And she suggested that others would, too. She knew of several women who needed to feel useful again.

It was now three years later, and they had managed to keep the house by taking in boarders: Vera Stafford, Maggie Rollins and the newcomer, Elizabeth Milford. Four elderly women who had been alone and lonely were now part of Lindsey's family.

"Maggie took the twins to the playground," Lindsey informed Vera. "We thought your son might not understand their third-degree questioning. They'll be back in time for lunch. He should be up on the roof and out of their reach by then."

She accepted the other women's laughter with a rueful shrug. All of them were aware that Carrie

14

and Kelly were fascinated by the male of the species. The mailman had to bribe the twosome with lollipops in order to get out of the yard. Last week a magazine salesman had forgotten his sales pitch entirely when the two little girls had solemnly asked him if he would like to be their new daddy.

Preschool had been the source of their sudden realization that theirs was not the usual family. When they had witnessed the other children with their fathers, they had begun asking questions. Having no memory of Peter, two literal minds had decided that they had never had a daddy; they were determined to gain one. The episode with the salesman was a prime example of their forthright efforts toward that goal.

The older members of the all-female household thought the twins' thorough examination of every male who came into their sphere amusing, but Lindsey found it embarrassing. All it took for a man to qualify for the position of "daddy" was a promise not to spank. Lindsey's lips twitched when she thought about herself marrying the sixty-four-year-old mailman, a grandfather of six. She was not looking forward to having as an overnight guest a man who might find Carrie and Kelly's questions extremely rude. Someone who spent his time in laboratories, surrounded by silent samples of rock, might not appreciate the questions asked by two little chatterboxes.

Actually, she was surprised that Marcus Stafford had volunteered to come at all. Vera had lived with them for more than six months and he had never once come for a visit. The elegant-looking older woman had explained that he was out of the country, made sure they knew how often she received a letter, and regaled them with the details of his travels. There had even been one trans-Atlantic phone call that set the entire household into an uproar, but Lindsey knew from painful personal experience that letters and occasional phone calls didn't replace the presence of a loved one. She herself had few letters and the memory of even fewer phone calls received from Peter when he had been too busy to come home. He had assured her that his absences were going to insure their future standard of living. But by concentrating all of his energy on their future, he had denied them both the simple pleasures to be found in the present and his death had cancelled their future forever.

Lindsey dragged her thoughts back to the present. "I'm going to put up the ladder. I don't know if I've bought enough shingles, so I'll take a look at the roof." She took one last bite of her roll, quickly licking the sticky remains from her fingers and lips. "I hope Mr. Stafford can get started before the twins get back. I can already hear them begging to go up on the roof."

"Call him Marcus," Vera insisted. "He's not that much older than you."

"He isn't?" Lindsey's brows rose with surprise. For some reason she had pictured Marcus Stafford as a short, bookish man, slightly balding, with the beginnings of a middle-aged spread thickening his waist. Vera had never described her son's physical

characteristics or mentioned his age, only his itin-
erary and details of his work.

"Well, a few years older," Vera agreed. But she
still insisted that Lindsey be less formal when
meeting him. He would feel foolish being referred
to as Mr. Stafford, Vera assured her. "He feels he
knows you from all of my letters. I told him all
about you and your girls. He refers to them as
Snow White and Rose Red. He's most anxious to
meet you, my dear."

Lindsey grinned. Hearing that the man had the
touch of the fanciful about him came as a relief.
Perhaps it would not be so difficult having him
around the house for two days. Carrie and Kelly
loved listening to a good fairy tale, and maybe
Marcus Stafford would consider telling them the
tale of the two princesses he had compared them
to. That is, if he wasn't so totally exhausted from a
day spent pounding shingles and applying pitch to
all the joints that he couldn't see to read.

"I'm looking forward to meeting him, too. Marcus it is," Lindsey said as she let herself out the
screened back door. She wandered down the
tarred drive to the front of the house, avoiding
the small pebbles to protect her bare feet. The
aluminum ladder was lying parallel to the house.
She bent down to lift it, relieved to find that it
wasn't too heavy. A few minutes later, she had it
propped up against the house, making sure the
metal feet were firmly planted in the soft soil of the
flower beds that surrounded the house.

She looked up at the roof, mentally counting the

bundles of shingles she had purchased the day before, hoping they were enough but needing to be sure. The stores would be closed tomorrow, and if she wanted the job done this weekend, she had to buy anything else that was needed today. She had been putting off the survey of the roof, thinking Marcus Stafford would arrive before it was necessary for her to climb up the ladder herself. She hadn't said anything to Vera, but the man was already hours late. He was supposed to have been busy on the roof before the twins woke up this morning, but since he was not, she had sent them off so they wouldn't bother him when he did arrive. It was beginning to look as if they would get back before he showed up.

She bit her lip and placed one sweaty hand on either side of the ladder. Her legs felt shaky as she carefully placed her bare feet on the first rung and started to climb. Every vibration she felt made her think she was about to fall.

Her crazy neurosis about heights dated back to when she was six and had climbed a tree after a pet cat. She had been unable to get back down and sat for hours in the pouring rain clutching the slippery branches of an old elm tree until help had finally arrived. She had never cheerfully lifted her feet off the ground since then.

When she reached the roof, she took a reassuring hold on the metal gutter, using both hands. She refused to look at the ground and see how high she had climbed. She began counting the missing or cracked weather-silvered shingles, beginning with the highest place near the chimney and working back down. When she finished her count of one side of the roof, she decided to climb back down and take the coward's way out. She should get up on the roof to count the missing shingles on the other side, but there was simply no way she could make herself do that. She would just multiply the amount missing by two and pray the number would be sufficient to cover the back side of the roof.

She groped behind herself with one bare foot, reaching for the next rung down on the ladder. She automatically glanced to locate the step, which proved to be a grave mistake. Her eyes dropped to the ground with a sickening visual jolt. Terra firma was a million miles below.

Her brain began swirling as her heart started pounding in panic. She hugged the ladder with both arms, closing her fingers into a vise where they met in the middle. She closed her eyes and held on for dear life. What should she do? She was too petrified to move; a scream for help would only terrify the two women in the kitchen, who couldn't do a thing about her predicament.

Think, you nitwit! she inwardly chided. Climb down the same way you climbed up and stop behaving like an idiot. No matter what she told herself, she couldn't seem to let go of the ladder. Her hands refused to unlock from their death grip; her toes were curled around the rung and a painful cramp was forming in each foot's arch.

A deep male voice shot up from below her. "How does it look up there?" The man grasped the ladder and placed a foot on the bottom rung, and Lindsey let out a small scream of utter terror as she felt the ladder shudder.

She made a panic-stricken grab for the gutter and cried, "I'm going to fall!"

2

Hold on!" the authoritative voice ordered. Lindsey was too petrified to do anything but obey. She squeezed her eyes shut, concentrating on gripping the gutter so she wouldn't fall. The man was going to make the ladder crash to the ground, she just knew it! It felt like a lumbering bear was climbing up after her.

"Take it easy, Rose Red. I'll soon have you down." The rich baritone voice was soft in her ear as her shaking body was covered from behind with a reassuring male form. His hands came down on hers, dwarfing them with long fingers that were gently trying to pry hers loose from their paralyzed grip on the gutter.

"Trust me, honey," the voice soothed, and miraculously, Lindsey found herself responding to the simple commands of her rescuer.

"I've got you and I won't let you go," he promised, and one hard arm clamped around her slim waist. He made sure her feet were placed firmly on the rungs, and he kept her body enclosed between himself and the ladder. They moved down together, one rung at a time. She allowed his strong hands to manipulate her and kept her eyes firmly shut, unable to look anywhere without succumbing to the churning nausea inside her.

"I'm right here. You can't fall," he reassured her, and she leaned gratefully against his strength.

It seemed to take an eternity, but at last her feet were planted on solid ground. Her rescuer turned her around to face him with two hands spanning her waist.

"You must be Kelly."

A boyish grin, complete with deep dimples, creased the rugged-looking face staring down at her. He had to be Marcus Stafford, but looked nothing like she had imagined Vera's son. He was apparently in his mid-thirties. His silver-blond hair fell in a wave over a broad forehead. His smoothly carved nose and well-defined lips added emphasis to the arrogant, square jaw and stubborn, jutting chin. Lindsey was too shaken to speak as he reached out a finger and lifted her chin. She found herself staring into the most incredibly sky blue eyes she had ever seen.

"If your mother had wanted you up on that roof, she wouldn't have asked me to come, now would she?" His voice held a mixture of adult censure and male amusement.

Lindsey barely registered the words as she took a step back to free her chin. She gazed in disbelief at the powerfully built man, bemused with the knowledge that she had recently leaned against him like a wilting flower. His shoulders were massive, the heavy muscles easily discernible beneath a faded blue T-shirt. Her gaze traveled lower and took in the narrow waist and hips of an athletic male body in its prime. A pair of tight blue Levi's molded muscular thighs and left little to the imagination. Without thinking, she blurted, "You aren't our geophysicist?"

His rumbling laughter jerked her gaze back to his face, her disbelief apparent in her wide-eyed gaze. "Marcus Stafford, rock and soil specialist extraordinaire," he introduced himself, clearly laughing at her. "I wasn't expecting Mrs. Delaney's daughter to be a sexy little number like you, either. Older than I expected, too." He made a curious survey of their surroundings. "I can't wait to meet your twin sister."

If he were expecting a blond version of Lindsey to step out of the bushes, he was in for an awful disappointment. His misconception about her identity was laughable, but she couldn't find the words to set him straight. It had been years since she had heard herself described as "sexy" by a member of the opposite sex, and she was having difficulty assimilating his assessment of her. In an unconsciously feminine reaction, she brushed a stray strand of hair off her face and hastily tucked her top back into the waistband of her shorts. She began to blush when he quirked his lips at her.

"Don't worry, sweetheart, you look great from any angle." He looked up the ladder with a wistful expression. "Especially that one, but I don't think you'd better try that again.

Totally disconcerted, Lindsey groped for the right words. She didn't know if she wanted to slap his grinning face or run away from the assessing blue eyes roaming familiarly over her figure, lingering overlong on her shapely bare legs. He was a predator, blatant and conceited—a "macho" man to the core! She was still thinking about the best approach to take with him when he took her arm and began guiding her toward the front steps.

"I think you're still a bit shaken," he decreed. "Let's go find my mother and yours and get you something cool to drink. Your mom wanted me up on that roof long before now, and although I'd like to while away a few more minutes with you, I did volunteer to start work. I've lost some valuable daylight hours as it is."

His indulgent tone rankled. She was not a child to be placated with a cool drink, and she couldn't wait to see his face when Vera introduced them. She hid a smile by ducking her head down—a seemingly submissive action. "Thank you for helping me," she said primly, firmly disengaging her arm from his grasp and taking the lead as they walked into the house.

"At your age, I'm surprised you still live at home

with your mother," he mocked, following much too closely behind her. "But I'm sure you benefit from the cozy setup your mother's got going here."

He was puzzled when his taunting was met with total silence. He had expected her to retaliate, give some flimsy excuse for why she was still being supported by her mother. Since she was home at this time of day, she certainly didn't hold down a full-time job. It looked as if she had no more qualms about accepting monetary help from the boarders than did her mother. It rankled him that her low, mellow voice affected him as intoxicatingly as good brandy. He savored the sound of it and wanted to hear it again.

"Your sister lives at home too, I gather?" At her continued silence, he took a different tack. "Is she as beautiful as you?"

Lindsey stopped dead in her tracks. Enough was enough. She was not surprised when he bumped into her and was unmoved by the slightly dazed expression on his face. He brushed his errant hair out of his eyes and cocked his head to one side in expectation.

"We appreciate your volunteering to help us, Mr. Stafford, but that gives you no right to make these outrageously personal comments. I wasn't expecting Vera's son to be an incorrigible flirt. We barely know one another, so I'd appreciate it if you kept your opinions to yourself."

"On the contrary," Marcus disagreed flashing an amused grin. "I feel as if I've known you for months. Let's see. You're accident-prone. Last month you took a spill on roller skates and had to have a few stitches taken in your chin." He studied her carefully and added, "I'm glad to see it left no scar."

Oblivious to Lindsey's struggles to keep a straight face, he continued. "You have a reckless nature that worries both your mother and mine. I even know that you have a tendency to pout when things don't go your way—a rather immature trait for one your age." A touch of frost edged his tone. "One evening a few weeks ago you ran off with one Billy Taylor without telling anyone where you'd gone. My mother wrote to tell me she had been worried sick about you. At her age, she shouldn't have to deal with that kind of anxiety, and while I'm here I plan to make sure she won't have to. I hope that's clear to you, Rose Red. You may think you're old enough to come and go without answering to anyone, but obviously our two mothers don't agree. Since you live under your mother's roof, I think it only fair that you extend to her the respect and consideration the woman deserves." His demeanor had grown steadily more parental as he loomed over her, lecturing what he obviously believed was a wayward daughter.

Lindsey's mouth had dropped open during his speech. She gaped at Marcus for a full five seconds before she began to laugh, clutching her sides as she shook with the force of her hilarity. The enormity of his misjudgment was the most humorous thing she had heard in a good long time. Her fit of laughter didn't amuse him, however. The fierce look on his handsome face made her laugh all the harder. The noise she was making brought both Vera and Althea from the kitchen, their faces alight with curiosity and pleasure.

Vera went immediately to Marcus and gave him a warm hug. He responded by slipping his arms around his petite mother, completely enveloping her with a bear hug that lifted her feet from the floor. He delivered an enthusiastic kiss to both her cheeks before releasing her.

When she had recovered from her greeting, Vera exclaimed, "I'm so glad you two have met and are getting along so well." Looking from Lindsey's animated face to Marcus, she was puzzled to see that Lindsey was the only one laughing.

Lindsey got a hold of herself while Vera introduced Marcus to Althea, impatiently waiting for the introduction that would knock Marcus Stafford totally off balance.

"And of course you two have met?" Vera patted Marcus' big hand and gestured to Lindsey.

"Actually, Vera, we haven't," Lindsey offered politely. "Mr. Stafford rescued me from the top of the ladder a few minutes ago, but we haven't introduced ourselves." She couldn't wait for him to discover who she was and to see his reaction. "I was up counting up how many shingles would be needed and couldn't get back down."

"Oh dear, how frightening," Vera cried. "Well, I'm glad Marcus arrived to help you, Lindsey. I know how frightened you are of heights."

"Lindsey?" There was the perfect amount of

stunned suspicion in Marcus' voice, and Lindsey's retaliatory smile lit up her whole face. She didn't go so far as to extend him a welcoming hand of greeting for fear he might break it, but she did nod her dark head decorously.

"I'm Lindsey Delaney," she announced with enjoyment. "I appreciate your concern for my daughter Kelly, but you've worried needlessly. She's just four years old and the worldly Billy Taylor only recently had his fifth birthday. He enticed Kelly to his sandbox with the promise of a root beer Popsicle, but they were both found quite soon thereafter."

To his credit, Marcus handled her pronouncement with considerable aplomb. His brows rose and a light pink tinged his cheeks, but his voice was calm when he spoke. "It seems I must readjust my thinking, Mrs. Delaney." He dipped his silver-maned head in a curt return of her nod. "So you are neither Snow White nor Rose Red, but their mother."

Placing an arm over his mother's shoulders, he gathered Vera tightly to his side. His blue eyes held a peculiar gleam as he scanned his mother's face. Lindsey wondered what was being said in their silent communication and got some idea when Marcus spoke again.

"You omitted a few pertinent facts, Mother. Perhaps I misunderstood the conversation we had last week when I got back into town."

Lindsey was mystified when Vera's lips twitched and she apologized for any misunderstanding. At the same time, she made it sound as if Marcus were a great deal to blame for misinterpreting her descriptions of the Delaney family. Lindsey couldn't wait to get Vera alone to find out exactly what the woman had said about her and the twins. She glanced up and caught a calculating expression on her grandmother's face. Althea was sizing up Marcus Stafford and finding him much more than adequate. Lindsey groaned inwardly and cast Althea a pleading look, which did absolutely no good.

"Come into the kitchen, Marcus dear; Lindsey has baked some delicious cinnamon rolls. I know you'll want a snack before climbing up on that roof." Althea stepped forward and took Marcus' other arm. The large man was promptly escorted into the kitchen by the two petite ladies. Lindsey followed resolutely behind, determined to nip any further matchmaking in the bud.

She hoped Marcus was unaware that he was being led to the romantic trough by two skillful women who still imagined that the way to a man's heart was through his stomach. Why hadn't she seen this coming? Vera, Maggie and Althea had been trying to get her to "catch" a man for herself for a long time. She imagined they'd thought Vera's son perfect for the part.

Scowling furiously, she watched as he was escorted to a kitchen chair like a king being guided to the throne. His two white-haired ladies-in-waiting burst into wreaths of smiles when he complimented Lindsey on her culinary talent and swallowed a mouthful of warm bread.

"Frozen from the bakery," she insisted and followed the denial with, "Whenever you are ready, Mr. Stafford, the supplies you requested are on the porch."

He took one last gigantic bite of his roll and smiled at Althea and his mother. "Better start earning my bread," he quipped good-naturedly, making Lindsey feel churlish for having rushed him. He stood and walked to the swinging door separating the kitchen from the dining room, then held it open and gestured to Lindsey to go ahead of him.

"Call me Marcus. And I can't wait to see what will be thawed out for lunch," he remarked low enough that only she could hear. Lindsey recognized the challenge, and forced herself not to flinch when her body brushed his as she passed through the door. He had deliberately allowed only limited space between himself and the frame, and she could not refuse the dare. The small skirmish didn't go unnoticed by the two women left behind, and Lindsey grimaced when she heard their faint laughter through the closed door. She stiffened her spine and led the way back to the porch.

It was going to be a very long weekend, exactly as she had feared, but not for the same reasons. Marcus Stafford was not shy, bookish, short or balding, but a compelling male who exuded vitality with every breath. She wished for a magic wand that could change him back into the inconsequential man she had imagined he would be. Having no magical power to call upon, she decided to be as honest as she could and explain that she wasn't on a campaign to ensnare an eligible male and expected nothing from him but a re-shingled roof.

She launched into her no-fault explanation as soon as they were safely out of earshot. "Marcus, I apologize for my grandmother's not so subtle matchmaking. I want you to know that I've never baked a homemade cinnamon roll in my life and I had no idea that those two would throw me at you. I hope you weren't embarrassed."

She ended on a rather breathless note that made him smile. "You've made two very interesting statements." Marcus bent down and lifted a bundle of roofing shingles onto his shoulder. He was expecting her to accompany him out of the porch down the front steps and into the yard. She did, wanting to find out what he meant by his ambiguous statement. She watched him place the bundle on the ground beside the ladder, then turn to tease her with his glorious blue eyes.

"First, my interest in you had already been piqued before I met your charming grandmother." He inspected the two blotches of color in her cheeks with detached interest. "Secondly, the thought of being thrown at you hardly embarrasses me. I'm fully prepared to enjoy it immensely, and if those two dears don't help, I may take matters into my own hands."

"What?" Lindsey sputtered, her face burning. "What are you saying?" Warm brown flames flickered beneath her long lashes as she digested his outrageous announcement. Stupidly, she stood in incredulous shock as he took a step closer and gazed directly into her flashing eyes.

"Gaining *your* interest in me is much more to the point. I don't imagine I'll require my mother's help to achieve that." Two large hands clamped around her arms and drew her to him, taking little notice of her efforts to free herself. "Your mouth is open, Mrs. Delaney." He lowered his voice, teasingly. "I appreciate it."

Lindsey's small scream of outrage was muffled by the searing impact of his hard mouth on hers. He took full advantage of her astonishment to invade the soft warm interior of her mouth with his probing tongue.

It was a devastatingly thorough, claim-staking endeavor, designed to leave her trembling with reaction, an inspired assault meant to spark her interest, and Lindsey could not claim it had not accomplished what was intended. She was aware of Marcus Stafford with every muscle, nerve and bone in her body, aware of the denim-clad thighs brushing against her bare legs, aware of the massive muscles of his chest that burned her through the thin material of her tank top, aware of his plundering, hard mouth that intrigued her vulnerable lips with teasing torrents of delight.

When she could no longer hide her unwilling response to his kiss, melting toward him like soft metal beneath a welder's torch, he lifted her feet off the ground, then set her down away from him.

"Having successfully gained your interest, I'll get back to work."

Lindsey was amazed at the shudders of response that shook her. Being without intimate male contact for three years had to be the only reason she was overreacting like this to a single kiss. She was shaking like a quivering bowl of jelly and her skin felt flushed with fever. Unconsciously her limpid brown eyes sought the man who had caused this devastation of the senses. Marcus was striding quickly up the front porch steps, his blond hair gleaming as the morning sun highlighted the shimmering color. He disappeared through the ornately fretted screen door, but Lindsey could hear him gathering the tools she had laid out for him to use.

She couldn't just keep standing here, looking like a small banty hen whose feathers had recently been ruffled by a flamboyant crowing cock, but that was exactly how she felt. He was so big, so overwhelming, and she felt helpless and vulnerable. She had to get rid of him, and soon. He was much too dangerous, totally outrageous, and she had no intention of becoming a victim of this kind of impetuous onslaught again. In his arms she had discovered that she was far too assailable. She wouldn't be able to withstand him for long. She had lost her head completely and yearned for more than his kiss. It was crazy, unthinkable, and she refused to give him full credit for her wanton reaction.

Although she had gone out with several men

since Peter's death, she had had no intimate relationship with any of them. She had responded to Marcus' embrace out of sheer instinct and the need for a man's touch. It would not, could not, happen again. She didn't want a man interfering with her peace of mind. She was perfectly happy with her life as it was. Marcus Stafford would soon find out that she wasn't another lonely widow eager to accept passion from the first man who offered, no matter what he expected from her after her response to his kiss.

Lindsey took several calming breaths, then glanced around her, aware for the first time since Marcus had taken her into his arms that he had kissed her in broad daylight. Anyone passing by could have seen them. This was a small town and she was well known; she taught second grade at the local elementary school. Traffic had been minimal this morning, thank goodness, and she hoped the tall spirea hedge and the graceful willow tree had shielded them from curious eyes.

Crossing her fingers that word was not spreading through the town that the young "Widow Delaney" had been boldly kissing a man in the middle of the morning, she walked deliberately toward the ladder, determined to inform Marcus that there would be no repeat of the scene. She crossed her arms over her chest to hide the still taut nipples that showed beneath her thin jersey top. Why hadn't she worn a bra today? She struggled to make her features expressionless, all the while glancing furtively about as if expecting the town gossips to descend upon her at any moment.

Marcus came off the porch carrying another bundle of shingles on his shoulders, a carpenter's apron tied around his lean waist and a hammer dangling in one hand. He took no notice of Lindsey's belligerent stance as he approached the ladder. "Hold this for a minute, would you?" He held out the hammer, and she took it without thinking. He then took a firm grasp on the ladder with one hand and lifted his foot up on the first rung.

"Wait!" Lindsey ordered firmly. "I don't want you to ever do anything like that to me again!"

The impact of glacial blue eyes frozen on her pale face was worse than his terse pronouncement. "I certainly won't."

The steely decisiveness in his voice pricked her with the force of a knife, and she deflated like a thin-skinned balloon. Her carefully guarded defenses shattered, she stammered, "But . . . I thought you liked—I thought you wanted me. . . ." Being found wanting in their exchanged kiss was a blow to her ego that had come out of nowhere, and she was unable to hide her reaction.

Wounded brown eyes searched his face, widening as his granite expression softened and his blue eyes lit up warmly. The now familiar grin stretched wide and flashed across his tanned face. "Well . . . if it means so much to you, then I will as often as you'll let me."

As soon as she registered the neat trap he had

laid for her and how easily and blindly she had walked into it, he readjusted the bundle on his shoulder and began climbing the ladder. "Oh!" She had an unholy urge to shake the metal frame until he fell off and landed on his fat head in the flower bed. Her temper boiled up and over, and she couldn't hold back. She kicked at a lump of earth with an outraged bare foot. "Arrogant, conceited, hateful, despicable—" Her low voice listed the adjectives that could be applied to Marcus Stafford, and he was back on the ground before she had completed her verbal accounting.

He took the hammer out of her clutched fingers and scampered back up the ladder out of her reach, reciting a list of his own in a humor-filled voice. "Beautiful, leggy, stacked, kissable—" He was still enumerating when she stumbled away from the ladder and ran swiftly into the house, letting the screened porch door bang loudly in her wake. She marched down the center hall and into the kitchen to pour herself a tall glass of pink lemonade.

Taking the drink with her, she went to the front parlor and plumped down on one end of the camel-backed love seat in the bay. A colorful pattern formed on the dusky rose carpeting as the sunlight streamed through the stained-glass transoms, but Lindsey took no notice. The lemonade brought her body temperature down, but did nothing to quench the raging inferno of her temper.

"That . . . that man!" she muttered emphatically under her breath. She drained her glass and punched one of the throw pillows scattered across the back of the mahogany-trimmed Duncan Phyfe settee.

"Well, I can't sit here all day fuming about him!" she declared as she rose to her feet and made her way back to the kitchen with her empty glass.

3

Rinsing her glass and turning to place it in the dishwasher, Lindsey fought with her smoldering anger when Vera boldly asked what she thought of her son. "Your son . . . Vera, he is . . ." She couldn't remember the last time she had felt any emotion as strong as what she was feeling for Marcus. She couldn't even define it. He had aroused both her temper and desire at the same time, leaving her off balance and unnerved.

"He certainly is," Vera agreed cheerfully, keeping her back to Lindsey in order to hide her wide smile. "I was forty years old when I had Marcus. He was my first and my last. His father died soon after, and I'm afraid I simply doted on Marcus. You can see that he has a rather high opinion of himself. It's not exactly conceit," she attempted to explain. "Marcus is simply enchanted with everything in life, including himself. Even as a small boy he was enthusiastic over the least little thing. Has he bowled you over, luv?"

"Not on your life!" Lindsey declared loudly, hoping her voice would drift up through the rafters and reach the hateful man working overhead. "It would take more than an adolescent bear of a man to knock me for a loop." She couldn't help glaring up at the ceiling, her cheeks flushed with temper as she lifted her empty glass and saluted Vera.

"He's an awful tease and a flirt. Always was," Vera agreed complacently, going to the refrigerator to remove the cold cuts they had planned for lunch. She continued, "Even as a boy, he charmed his way into everyone's affections, but as for the teasing . . . Maybe he's so used to talking to rocks he's forgotten that people have softer exteriors."

"He talks to rocks?" Althea frowned and glanced up. "He seemed quite sensible to me."

Her serious tone won smiles from both of the other women, and Vera chuckled. "At thirty-three and still unmarried, he's not nearly as sensible as I'd hoped. I thought I'd have several grandchildren by now."

"So! You *were* matchmaking," Lindsey accused, waggling a finger beneath the older woman's nose without rancor. "Give it up Vera, for both our sakes. As far as grandchildren, you will always have Carrie and Kelly. They've adopted you. They'll win

Elizabeth over, too, if she'd come out of her room once in a while." Lindsey's face grew serious as her thoughts changed to include their newest boarder.

"It's a shame." Althea brought a plate of freshly baked bread to the table and began slicing it, warming to the subject they had been discussing for days. "I've known Liz for years, and I'd never have expected her to handle Harry's death like this. She's young yet, and her training as a registered nurse could be put to good use. Given up, that's what she's done."

"She told me yesterday that it's her turn to die. I've never heard such negative thinking." Vera began paring apples to place beside the large cut of cheddar cheese on a tray. "Her daughter couldn't take her in, and Liz should be glad. We can't count on our children to make something out of our lives. I won't have Marcus worried over me when he takes a project out of the country and is gone for months. Now I've got my own projects going and don't spend my time worrying over him every second. It's a blessing."

Lindsey had gotten her boarders involved in a senior citizens' group associated with their church. Each week the ladies gathered to work on charity projects that helped both themselves and the needy.

"Yes, it is." Althea reached for Lindsey's hand and squeezed it. "That's why it's such a joy to live here. I feel useful again. Don't you, Vera?"

"Overworked is more like it," Vera snapped playfully. "I have two quilts needing to be finished before the July Festival, besides all the canning I want to do."

Lindsey kept her comments in the same light vein. "I only keep you ladies around to serve me and the community. Also to cook, mend and look after the kids so that I can enjoy a life of leisure." Their banter came to an abrupt end as a loud hammering began on the roof.

Lindsey put her hands over her ears and rose from the table. "I'd better go tell Elizabeth what the noise is all about."

A few minutes later, she knocked on Elizabeth's bedroom door and waited for the feeble response from inside. Getting none, she opened the door to the darkened room and stepped in. "Sleeping in again?" She smiled at the frail woman lying with her head on the lace-edged pillow of the large brass bed. She crossed the room and opened the drapes, letting in the June sunshine. "Lunch is in an hour, Elizabeth. You remember that Vera's son is joining us today?" Lindsey asked, recalling that Elizabeth had the tendency to forget things if she weren't constantly reminded. The forgetfulness seemed more a refusal to involve herself in life than an actual inability to remember. She went to the bed and helped the woman sit up on the edge.

Elizabeth felt like a tiny, delicate bird. Her gray-streaked hair was tangled and uncombed although clean from Lindsey's having washed it the day before. "You wanted to wear the blue dress, didn't you?" she reminded, going to the closet to take the dress down from its hanger. She laid out the clothes

Elizabeth needed to put on, then picked up a hairbrush and returned to the bed. She chattered brightly as she brushed Elizabeth's hair away from her pale, lined face. "Vera's counting on us to make Marcus feel welcome."

"She's been a good friend," Elizabeth said in a dull voice, her gray eyes showing little interest. "I'm sure he's a nice boy." She waved Lindsey away with a dismissing hand, stood up and shuffled toward her dresser.

Sighing, Lindsey left the room and walked down the hall. The words, "He's a nice boy," echoed inside her head. Marcus was neither a boy nor nice, but she supposed he would appear that way to Elizabeth—if, that is, Elizabeth took any notice of him at all. Lindsey truly enjoyed the diverse group of older women who had come to live with her, but Elizabeth presented some unique problems—ones she was determined to overcome. Somehow she was going to get through to the woman, make her see that she still had plenty left to give, and many reasons to go on living.

Althea had raised Lindsey after the death of Lindsey's parents in a plane crash. Lindsey was accustomed to the idiosyncrasies of the elderly and appreciated the importance of family. She was glad that her children had an overabundance of grandmothers. After her marriage to Peter, she had lost touch somewhat with her own grandmother since Peter had made no attempt to hide his impatience when Althea was visiting.

Peter, too, had been an orphan, but unlike Lindsey, who had been lovingly reared by a grandmother, had been shuttled from foster home to foster home. Rather than longing for a family life because of his experiences, he had seemed indifferent to it. Lindsey had often thought that since he had felt so little love in his life, he somehow was incapable of extending it. Lindsey had ended up seeing Althea only on the major holidays and had missed her very much.

It was good to be with her again, good to share their relationship with others and see her children reap the rewards of wisdom provided by the elderly. Everyone, with the exception of Elizabeth, seemed to be flourishing from their unique household arrangement. They were a self-contained unit, and the last thing they needed was a disruptive male coming on the scene to throw everything out of kilter.

"Mommy!" Kelly's voice resounded up the stairs. "The worker-man says I have t' ask you if he can come down to eat lunch with us. He says he doesn't deserve a break yet. Can't he come down, Mommy? Can't he?"

Lindsey shook her head with annoyance. The disruption had already started. Kelly must be convinced that her mother was some kind of Simon Legree standing over the "worker-man" with a whip! Exasperated, she called back, "Tell Mr. Stafford he can join us for lunch and that it will be ready in about half an hour." She walked down the stairs and met her young daughters on the landing. Kneeling down, she scooped them both up in a big hug. "Are you two hungry after all that playing this morning?"

Kelly, who looked like a miniature Lindsey, began launching into a blow-by-blow description of their adventures on the playground. Carrie stood silently within the curve of her mother's arm, solemnly nodding her curly blond head in agreement. When Lindsey had heard about every trip the twins had made down the "giant" slide, all about the "mean" boy who had hogged the sandbox, and how Maggie had become cross when they had pretended to be monkeys hanging upside down on the jungle gym, Kelly began tugging on Lindsey in an effort to drag her to the kitchen.

"We're not supposed to call that worker-man Mr. Stafford. I asked Maggie what he would be if Vera was our real grandma and she said he'd be our uncle. So we asked him if we could call him Uncle Marcus."

Carrie decided it was her turn to speak. "He said he'd like to be our uncle because we're so pretty. He's nice, Mommy."

"Nice," Lindsey gritted, grateful the children were too young to pick up on her sarcastic tone. They entered the kitchen, where Maggie was being treated to a well-deserved cup of herbal tea.

"Couldn't keep them away from the 'worker-man' a minute longer," Maggie puffed, her ample bosom rising and falling. She placed both hands over her ears and shouted, "Sounds like progress, but I wish I needed a hearing aid so I could shut the thing off."

Lindsey thanked Maggie for taking the children off her hands and directed the twins to the bathroom off the kitchen to wash up, then told the group that Elizabeth was going to join them for lunch and was not surprised that everyone had been expecting her to stay up in her room.

Lindsey made no comment as she laid out the silverware and saw that the food was being served up on her good china. Marcus was a guest, an honored one, and she had to try to remember that.

Although they generally ate in the kitchen, lunch was being served in the large formal dining room. The food had been laid out on the large antique sideboard, and Vera filled each plate that was passed. Lindsey didn't enter the conversation, a bit startled that Marcus didn't take his seat until after he had escorted each female, the old and the young, to their chairs with a dashing show of gallantry. She managed to avoid his assistance and sat down at the head of the table, one twin on either side of her. Marcus had his hands full trying to manage a bite of his food between answering the questions posed by Althea, Vera, Maggie and the twins. Only Elizabeth and Lindsey offered little. While Elizabeth smiled shyly, apparently content to listen, Lindsey seethed at the sound of the booming male voice so alien to their household.

Dessert was a large wedge of lemon meringue pie. Marcus' boyishly eager enjoyment of it was noticed with pleasure by the house cook. Althea dimpled like a young girl when he complimented her on the pie and, pronouncing it the best he had ever had, begged for another piece.

By the end of the meal, he had four white-haired women and two preschoolers hanging on his every word. His rumbling laughter made Lindsey jump whenever she heard it, it was such an unfamiliar sound to ears tuned to the gentle tones of women. She had sensed his eyes on her several times during the meal, but she had stubbornly refused to meet his gaze. The less contact of any kind she had with him, the better. It would be far too easy to find herself enthralled by him.

"Can we go up on the roof and watch Uncle Marcus?" Kelly asked, eyeing her mother with hopeful brown eyes.

"I'm afraid not, honey," Lindsey returned automatically.

"I could hand him the nails," Kelly suggested, not yet ready to take no for an answer. Lindsey's sharp negative response was so unlike her that Kelly's pixie face crumpled and her lower lip quivered.

"Why don't you take your dolls out to the porch and play house," Lindsey soothed. "Then you can talk to . . . Marcus whenever he needs a break and has to come down from the roof." She got a begrudging nod from two disappointed little girls as they politely excused themselves and went to get their toys.

"I hope you don't mind." Lindsey eyed Marcus warily, uncertain whether he would be annoyed

46

with her for offering his time to her girls. Their undisguised interest would only get worse if she didn't give them the opportunity to question him.

"Not at all," Marcus replied and excused himself from the table. "May I have a word with you, Lindsey? In private?"

"Certainly," Lindsey agreed, not understanding what he needed to discuss without the others hearing.

He took her arm as he rounded the table and suggested they use the study he had seen when Vera had given him a tour before lunch. Lindsey walked with him down the center hall and into the small paneled room. She hid her astonishment when he closed the sliding oak doors behind them.

He seemed overwhelmingly tall all of a sudden, and Lindsey had an impulsive urge to back away from him. Her feelings were ridiculous. He probably had discovered some problem with the roof and wanted to discuss it without involving the others. She should be appreciating his consideration.

"I've cleared up a few things with my mother," he began, but she found her attention diverted to his trim waist as he hooked his thumbs in his tight jeans and leaned his shoulders back against the wall. "You've a pleasant living arrangement going here." He scanned her face, but Lindsey kept her face hidden as she hastily took a chair so she wouldn't be caught staring.

"That's right." Her voice sounded oddly defensive, and that infuriated her. What was the matter with her, anyway? Why should a simple statement of fact bother her? Maybe because she felt as if Marcus was behaving like he was cornering a weaker adversary. He had made a similar remark earlier in the day when he had thought she was Kelly. Lindsey was increasingly puzzled. Just what was he getting at? It was her turn to scan his face, but she found nothing in his expression to indicate his thoughts.

His voice was calm, and a rather sheepish grin appeared at the corners of his generous mouth. He said, "I thought you were a middle-aged widow running some kind of scam to finagle money out of rich older women. I was obviously wrong."

"Right again," she replied, this time her voice holding the perfect amount of assurance. She relaxed back against the wing of her chair. He was working up to an apology, and she was willing to accept it graciously. After all, he had only kissed her, and she was a mature woman who certainly wasn't going to be thrown by a single kiss.

"Have you wrapped yourself in this comfortable cocoon to feel safe from the outside world?" The probing question stole beneath her guard.

"What?" she asked, slightly dazed. "Why do you think you have the right to ask such a question?" She sat up ramrod straight in the chair. "You're a guest in my home, Mr. Stafford. I don't think I need answer your question."

"Just as I suspected," he shot back. "You're scared of anyone who might upset the boat, aren't you?" He gave her a glinting mocking glance from shrewdly narrowed eyes. "I'm glad you didn't turn out to be the woman I'd expected. I came down here intent on preventing any more taps into my mother's resources."

"You what?" Lindsey stood up, bristling, her brown eyes signaling both disbelief and outrage. His booming laugh did little to soothe her aroused temper but did serve to keep her quiet while he continued.

"When I saw two designer dresses charged to my mother's account, I became suspicious. Then when she wrote to me for funds to re-roof your entire house I thought it wise to get down here fast, so I volunteered to fix the roof myself and save us all some money."

Lindsey's hands clenched and unclenched in fury. "Oh!" she exclaimed. "You needn't bother. I'll get someone else to fix this roof. Your mother purchased two beautiful dresses for my girls for their birthday. I didn't ask her to buy them anything, and I didn't ask her to provide the funds for the roof, either. I don't need favors from either you or your mother!"

"I know."

"Then why have you told me all this?" Lindsey exploded.

"I wanted to let you know that I now have my facts straight." Marcus sounded calm, unaffected by Lindsey's appalled fury. He gave her an indulgent smile. "I've discovered that you're a very courageous and special woman who doesn't realize what's she's been missing by burying herself away from the world. Something has to be done about you, Lindsey Delaney."

His uncanny knack for deflating her ire with a compliment was confusing. She didn't know if she was angry, pleased, or simply out of her depth. What did he mean, something had to be done about her? He grinned again, seeing that she had no idea where he was going with the conversation. "I'm going to make you see things a bit more clearly. Someone has to knock you off the complacent shelf you've been sitting on for the last three years."

Lindsey had had enough. She began moving toward the door, intent on ignoring his outrageous statements. "I think it best for me to hire someone else to work on my roof. I'll explain to your mother that our arrangement didn't work out."

His hand reached out for her wrist as she swept past him. "It's working out very well," he disagreed, pulling her away from the door. "I keep all my promises, Lindy. I promised to fix your roof and I intend to. I also promised to kiss you whenever you let me . . . like now."

With one tug, he had her falling against him, his large hands curving over her shoulders to hold her steady. His blue eyes caressed her face, studying her pink mouth with undisguised hunger. "I'm not letting you kiss me!" she exclaimed breathlessly, struggling uselessly in his strong grasp.

"Aren't you?" he murmured, capturing her arm

behind her back and gathering her to his chest. "Your mouth is a delightful invitation that I accept." His lips preyed along the delicate line of her jaw, nibbling tiny bites of pleasure on his way to her mouth. His hands seemed to burn through her thin tank top to the smooth skin underneath as Lindsey swayed toward him, mesmerized, closing her eyes to hide the tumultuous feelings that were bubbling pleasurably inside her. "Aren't you?" he repeated and took her mouth.

She was enveloped by the massive male strength of him. A thousand wild sensations washed over her, engulfing her. Patiently, deliciously, his tongue coaxed a response from her, but she pulled her head away. "Please," she moaned as her body betrayed her, softening with invitation. Her struggles ceased and became the instinctive fluttering of a moth being coaxed to the flame. His mouth opened on hers, his tongue slid easily between her parted lips to make a slow foray through her mouth. He kissed her leisurely, the tip of his tongue gliding through the interior of her mouth, dancing and circling until she strained against him, driven by a feminine force compelled to find its masculine counterpart. As she was about to succumb to her desire to wrap her arms around him and bring him closer yet, he suddenly let her go.

"I'll be up on the roof when you want me again." He tapped the end of her nose with a gentle finger, smiling with both his eyes and his mouth.

"Of all the colossal conceit!" Lindsey managed,

though her lips were swollen by his all-consuming possession. "Out! Get out of here!" she raged, lifting her arm to swing it in an arc aimed at his face.

He caught her hand in midair, gently but firmly twisting her wrist to bring her palm to his lips. He pressed a tiny warm kiss in the very center and closed her fingers over it as if to hold it in place. "Pride goeth before a fall, Lindy. You've got to get back into the mainstream of life." His familiar grin taunted her frustration. "Somebody has to make sure you're properly rewarded for the help you've given some unique and wonderful people. I consider it my pleasant duty to give you a few of life's pleasures. You deserve them."

He promptly left the room, sliding the study doors closed behind him, leaving Lindsey to digest the most incredible statement she had ever heard.

4

Lindsey massaged the small of her back to relieve the nagging ache. She bent over and unplugged the vacuum, then wound the cord and dragged the heavy upright to its accustomed place in the walk-in hall closet. She brushed her perspiring brow with the back of her hand and grimaced at the continued incessant pounding going on overhead. She had taken out her frustration with Marcus on the upstairs carpets, the noisy vacuum camouflaging her whispered epithets at the man working up on the roof. Stoked by her anger, adrenalin flowed through her body, giving her the energy required to move the heavy furniture as she cleaned every last inch of the second floor.

Now, hours later, her knit top was clinging

damply to her breasts, wisps of hair strayed untidily about her heat-flushed face and her bare legs were coated with a thin film of dust. She was in desperate need of a shower, both to rid herself of the dirt she had accumulated during her efforts and to cool down her still flaring temper.

The staccato beat of a hammer kept time with the intermittent surge of water from the antiquated plumbing in her shower. Usually she was tolerantly amused by the idiosyncrasies of the ancient plumbing, but today the on and off rhythm, joined with Marcus' hammering, seemed to mock her and make her head pound. As far as she was concerned, one of the greatest pleasures life could hold was taking a relaxing, cleansing shower in peaceful silence—and with consistently heavy water pressure! She couldn't relax when her thoughts were centered on the arrogant male perched not far above her head on the roof.

With every stroke of the hammer he held in his hand, she formed an image of the muscled sinews of his arms, the power in his large hands and the gentleness of his fingertips upon her body. She had to stop thinking like that! What's the matter with you, Lindsey? she chided herself. Maybe it's true that you're a frustrated widow crazed for a man's touch! Angrily, she yanked back the shower curtain and stepped out of the high-sided claw-foot tub, convincing herself that her reaction to Marcus was no different than if it had been any other man who had kissed her so thoroughly. Pure glandular reaction. That's all it is! After all, I'm still a young woman, she reminded herself.

She toweled herself briskly, applying an overly generous amount of her favorite dusting powder in the hope that the delicate fresh scent would help her remain comfortable in the summer's heat. Marching into her bedroom, she paused before the closet, one hand clutching a towel, while she tried to think of something cool to slip on. The hammering had mercifully stopped, at least for a short time, and Lindsey could hear Marcus' deep voice answering the twins' chatter. When she heard his booming laugh, her curiosity got the better of her and she reluctantly went to the window to eavesdrop on their conversation.

"That old room is dark and spooky. My mommy's room is real pretty. You could share it with her," Kelly suggested enthusiastically.

As Lindsey swallowed a lump of appalled mortification, she heard Carrie add in a logical tone, "Her bed is *real* big. She doesn't mind sharing it."

"Oh, she doesn't?" was Marcus' response between chuckles.

Lindsey's embarrassment mounted as serious-minded Carrie enumerated all the reasons it would be a good idea for Marcus to share Lindsey's bed. "You can ask her, Uncle Marcus. She always lets us sleep with her when there's thunder. There's plenty of room. And it's nice 'cuz she always smells *so* good."

Lindsey had never moved faster. She grabbed

the first garment that met her hand when she reached into the closet. Pulling the red and white gingham shirred-top sundress over her head, slipping on fresh underwear and thrusting her feet into a pair of sandals, she raced down the hall and back stairs and into the kitchen.

Spying a pitcher of lemonade and glasses placed on a tray in readiness to be taken outside, she blessed whoever had made it for their foresight. It was the perfect excuse she needed to go outside and break up the conversation. Giving a breezy, "I'll take it," Lindsey picked up the tray and was through the swinging kitchen door and on her way to the front porch before any of the open-mouthed women seated around the table could make a comment.

All eyes centered on the swinging cafe doors. Althea was the first to speak. "She was wearing a dress."

"Her hair was all wet," Vera observed.

"She's wearing that dusting powder I gave her for her birthday," Maggie added.

All three women smiled at each other, murmuring in unison, "Hmmm."

Striving to appear casual, Lindsey surveyed the porch but didn't see either one of her daughters. Carrie's voice drifted through the screens from outside on the lawn. "You're not s'posed to do that, Kelly. Mommy'll get mad."

Kelly's answering response came from someplace close to the house—and high. "Uncle Marcus can't hear me if I'm down there."

Immediately, Lindsey put down the tray on a nearby wicker table and dashed for the screened door. Her heart was beating overly fast as she shouted, "Kelly!" rounding the house in time to see her reckless daughter lose her grip on the metal ladder. "Kelly!" She screamed as she watched in helpless horror as the small body plummeted to the ground, landing in a crumpled heap on the grass. In the few seconds it took for Lindsey to regain the use of her legs, Marcus had realized what had happened and was climbing down the ladder.

They reached Kelly at the same time. Instinctively, Lindsey reached out for her daughter, intending to gather her up, but she was prevented by a steely grasp on her arm and a barked command. "Don't touch her! Not until we see if any bones are broken."

Kelly was lying unconscious, face up, with her arms and legs flung out, one leg bent at an unnatural angle. "Carrie, get Elizabeth," Lindsey demanded in a choked voice as soon as she had seen the deathly pallor of Kelly's face. She could hear Carrie's frightened shouts as Marcus leaned over the tiny child to check her breathing. There was no need to fetch the other women; with Althea in the lead, they were all rapidly crossing the lawn.

Lindsey began calmly issuing orders, telling Vera to return to the house for a blanket, asking Maggie to call for an ambulance. Elizabeth knelt down and began running her hands over Kelly's still form.

In an authoritative voice that none of them had heard before, Elizabeth brushed Marcus aside.

"Give me some room. Don't worry, Lindsey, we won't let anything happen to our little girl." She reassured them with the information that Kelly's pulse was strong. But Lindsey wasn't appeased, terrified that her daughter remained oblivious to the flurry of activity going on around her.

"Mommy! Mommy!" Carrie's frightened voice broke through Lindsey's single-minded concern for her other daughter. A small hand was placed in her own.

She lifted Carrie into her arms and comforted her as she would have liked to comfort the little girl lying on the ground. "She'll be fine," she repeated over and over in an attempt to reassure the child in her arms as well as herself. She handed her over to Althea's waiting arms as the sound of a wailing siren drew closer. "You stay and take care of grandma while I take Kelly to the hospital. Doctor Ann will make Kelly all better, but she'll want me to be with her. Do you understand, sweetheart?" Large, round blue eyes registered her understanding, and with a slight nod of her curly blond head, Carrie went willingly into her great-grandmother's embrace.

The uniformed members of the emergency squad lost no time confirming Kelly's vital signs, supporting her injured leg in a temporary splint, then carefully placing her on a stretcher. Just before they lifted her into the waiting ambulance, Carrie wiggled out of Althea's arms and dashed to her sister's side. Placing a quick kiss on Kelly's cheek, she said softly, "You'll be all right, Kelly. Mommy said so."

Marcus handed a white-faced Lindsey into the back of the ambulance. "I'll follow in my car." His voice was gruff, conveying the deep emotion Lindsey couldn't allow herself to show. If she broke down now, she knew she would cry all the way to the hospital. Also, she had to think about Carrie. The diminutive, flaxen-haired girl thoroughly believed that whatever her mother told her was true, and Lindsey could not show by one tear that she doubted her own assurances. She nodded at Marcus and smiled encouragingly at Carrie and the others until the ambulance doors blocked them from her view.

The trip to Columbus was made swiftly. Lindsey clung to Kelly's hand while one of the medics monitored the dainty patient's vital signs during the trip, constantly reassuring Lindsey that they were steady and within normal range. Lindsey looked up once and was oddly reassured by the sight of Marcus' dust-covered jeep wagon following closely behind.

"Youngsters can take quite a fall and be all right within hours. Everything looks good, except I'm sure she's broken her leg, Mrs. Delaney." Lindsey turned to the voice of the man attending Kelly and recognized him as Dan Tibbels, father of one of her students during the past school year.

"Thank you, Dan. I'm sorry I didn't recognize you before."

"It's okay, you had your little girl on your mind. She sure is a pretty little thing. You know, my wife and I have only boys. We've always wished for a daughter." Dan's gentle voice went on, continually calm, but his eyes rarely left his small patient, and Lindsey sensed that he was doing his best to allay her anxiety. "My boy, Jeremy, sure liked having you for his teacher last year, and Mary and I are thankful that you gave him such a good year."

"Jeremy is a fine boy, Dan. It was a pleasure to have him in my class." Their small talk continued until the emergency vehicle came to a stop. Dan reached over to pat Lindsey's knee.

"She'll be in good hands here. This hospital is one of the best. You just stick close to me and we'll find out everything real fast. Dr. Ann is your doctor; she's already radioed that she's on her way. The hospital staff has been waiting for us."

Lindsey had only time to smile her gratitude. The back doors swung open and two white-uniformed attendants reached for the stretcher. Kelly was lifted out and carried through the wide doors of the hospital emergency room. Dan helped Lindsey down and guided her through the entrance and toward the waiting room with a promise that he would follow Kelly to emergency and report back to Lindsey as soon as he had any information.

As soon as she had given the clerk Kelly's medical history and the name of their insurance company and signed a release, Lindsey sank into one of the vinyl chairs and leaned back against the ceramic-tiled wall, unseeing of her surroundings, save the doors that had just closed behind Kelly's stretcher and Dan Tibbels's slender figure.

"Lindsey?" A vaguely familiar male voice broke through her dazed consciousness, and she looked up to the source.

Looking down at her, Marcus was overcome by the need to take her in his arms. Her large brown eyes looked so sad and fearful. Her hair was still damp, but hung in soft waves around her face, just brushing the top of her slender shoulders. He crouched down on his heels in front of her and took one of her limp, cold hands in his. "Can I get anything for you?" It was an inane question and he knew it, but was helpless to offer the one thing she wanted above all else—positive proof that her child was all right.

It felt so good to have her hand held in Marcus' large warm one. "Nothing, thank you, Marcus. They've taken her through those doors, and one of the medics will be out as soon as he knows something." Her voice was flat, devoid of all expression, and low, as if all her strength had been drained during the trip in the emergency van. Not letting go of her hand, Marcus straightened and took the chair next to hers.

They sat in silence, both watching the door, anxiously waiting for someone to come through and give them some news about Kelly. The minutes dragged slowly into nearly half an hour. Then Dan came through the doors. Both Lindsey and Marcus jumped up and rushed toward him.

Before Lindsey could utter one word, Dan began. "Dr. Ann says they're going to admit her for a day or more. She broke both bones in her lower right leg, and they'll have to set them."

"Is she still unconscious?"

"Most of the time. She bumped her head pretty good when she fell and has a concussion. They're taking her in to X ray right now to see if there's a skull fracture and get some pictures of her leg. Dr. Ann will stay with her; she should be out as soon as she's finished. Meanwhile, they want you to go to the business office and get Kelly admitted."

Lindsey tried to steel herself against the worst. Kelly had fallen so far. Skull fracture; it sounded so frightening. She must have started to sway. She felt her knees begin to wobble, then Marcus placed a supporting arm around her waist. This was no time to give in to the weakness of tears. She had to be calm. Trying to smile, she whispered her thanks to Dan.

"You're more than welcome, Mrs. Delaney. I'm sure that little gal will be awake and chirpin' before you know it." Awkwardly, he patted her shoulder. "Well, I've got to get back to Baldridge. You let us know how she's doing."

Marcus asked directions to the admitting office and steered Lindsey down the hall. "By the way, I think this belongs to you." He handed Lindsey her purse, with a slight grin. "It really doesn't go with my jeans."

His grin and light tone were almost her undoing as she received her straw bag from Marcus. When she realized how long he had been holding it and how ridiculous it looked tucked beneath his muscled arm, Lindsey smiled—her first genuine smile since the accident. "Pink just isn't your color," she teased shakily.

"I guess your grandmother wasn't thinking when she handed it to me," he quipped with a grin.

They arrived at the business office, and Lindsey was soon busy filling out the myriad of papers required to admit her daughter into the hospital. That finally done, Marcus cupped her elbow in his hand and accompanied her back to the waiting area. Seating her on one of the sofas, he went to fetch a cup of coffee for her, despite her protest that she wanted nothing. Minutes later, he returned carrying a styrofoam cup in each hand.

"I added a little cream, I hope you don't mind. You didn't say how you like it, and it looked mighty strong to me." He thrust the cup in her hands. "Anyway, it's warm. You look as if you could use a little warmth."

She wrapped her fingers around the warm cup and relaxed slightly. "Thank you, Marcus, Thank you for coming, too." Feeling a little uneasy with his calm solicitude, she added, "You don't have to stay. I'll be all right."

"No way. She wouldn't have climbed up if I hadn't been up on the roof talking to her. I feel responsible." He sat down beside her and leaned forward, resting his forearms on his thighs and holding the coffee between his knees. Looking at the lines of worry furrowed across his forehead, she realized that there was no hint of the arrogant, teasing man she had first met. Lindsey couldn't stop herself from reaching out to touch his broad shoulder.

"Oh, Marcus, you can't blame yourself. Kelly has always been absolutely fearless. She would have climbed up on that ladder no matter who was up there."

"Thanks, but I should have realized her voice was getting closer."

"You couldn't have done anything. I had already warned her several times to stay off the ladder. It's nobody's fault except mine for not watching her more closely. After all, I know what she's like."

He straightened, turned and grinned at her. Seeing her hand still resting on his shoulder, Lindsey quickly withdrew it, feeling embarrassed and thankful that he seemed oblivious to her light touch. "I suppose you do. According to Mom, she's in some kind of trouble most of the time. Sounds like the only way you could possibly keep her safe is to lock her up in a padded room. Maybe we'd both better stop accusing ourselves."

"You're right," she responded with another small smile. "I should be used to things like this with her by now. We've been stitching her up every now and then since she was a toddler. Only . . ." Her voice broke when the image of Kelly's pale, quiet face flashed across her brain. "She's never been unconscious before." She bit her lip and blinked back the tears.

Immediately, Marcus slid his arm around her

shaking shoulders and pulled her against him. "Hey, hey, she'll be awake soon. Tibbels didn't seem too worried. I asked a nurse about it while you were filling out all the papers, and she explained that unconsciousness isn't too unusual in trauma cases with young children. She said that as long as her breathing and other signs were normal, there probably wasn't too much to worry about." He placed his cup down on the table in front of them and took hers from her lifeless fingers. Then he completely enveloped her in his arms until her cheek was resting on his chest and one of his hands was lightly stroking her hair.

She relaxed against him, grateful to have someone to lean on after such a long time. She had had to be both father and mother to the twins, be their strength without being able to call upon anyone else for herself. She could hear his steady heartbeat beneath her cheek and allowed the heat from his powerful body to gradually soothe her chilled one. He smelled so masculine, a hint of sunshine emanating from his cotton shirt, mixed with his own musky scent and a fresh, citrus men's cologne. She let a few tears flow before she pulled away and fumbled in her purse for a tissue to wipe her eyes and nose.

He let her go reluctantly, and handed her the cup of coffee. She took a sip, grimacing slightly at the bitter strong taste.

"Thanks, I'm sorry. I don't usually break down like that."

"It's okay. You're entitled to a few tears. I'll admit

to a few on the way up here. You have two very lovely daughters. I can see that Kelly is the talker, but I sense that there's a lot going on inside that little blond head of Carrie's. She doesn't say much, but when she does, it's worth hearing."

Painfully recalling every detail of the conversation she had overheard between Marcus and the twins, Lindsey turned to him, searching for the mocking glint she expected to see in his blue eyes. There was none, and she loosened the grasp she had unconsciously held on her cup. Thankful that he was not going to bring up her daughter's suggested sleeping arrangements, Lindsey launched into a description of the twin's antics.

At one point, when Marcus stopped her with a roar of laughter, she thought that it was to his credit that he appeared so genuinely interested in two four-year-olds. Whatever his reason, she was grateful that he had started her talking and helped her endure the wait.

Feeling embarrassed about going on and on about her children, Lindsey stopped. "This must be boring you to death. I'm sorry, but you asked for it. Now you know you should never ask a mother about her children—she'll tell you."

"I'm not bored. Mom has written so much about them since she moved in with you that I almost felt as if I knew them. Except, as you recall, I was ignorant of their ages." Sobering, he offered quietly, "I'm sorry about all my misunderstandings, Lindsey. It means a lot to me that my mother is so happy. You and your children have given her a new lease on life. She's been feeling pretty depressed in the last few years, and since my job takes me away a lot, I've been worried about her. I said before that you're a very special woman, and you are. There can't be many in your circumstances who would bother to help lonely older women—especially three who aren't even related to you." His eyes held hers as he softly pronounced, "You're an angel."

Lindsey tore her gaze away and flushed. "There's nothing heavenly about me. I need them as much as they need me. Your mother is a wonderful person, as are all the other women who live with us. They're the angels."

Before she knew it, she had explained all her circumstances to Marcus, that she would have lost her house if it were not for her boarders, and how much they helped her with the care of the twins while she was teaching.

He studied her face for long moments when she finished. "You really don't understand what you're doing for them, do you?"

"I . . . I just explained how much they help me. It's *I* who probably benefit the most, just as you originally suspected."

"No, Lindsey Delaney. You make them feel useful. You give them a reason to get up in the morning. You do need them, and that's just what each of them wants—to feel needed. My own mother seems years younger. She's happy. You're responsible for that happiness, you and those little girls of yours. Thank you."

His eyes locked with hers again, and she felt for the first time some understanding of this man. She realized that maybe he understood her a little better than she understood herself.

The swish of the doors broke the intensity of the moment, and both turned quickly to see a nurse striding briskly toward them.

"Mrs. Delaney?"

Lindsey stood immediately. "I'm Mrs. Delaney. How is my daughter?"

The nurse smiled and walked toward her. "We'll be bringing her out in a few minutes. She's going to be just fine. Dr. Martinez will explain everything to you." As if on cue, the doors opened again and Ann Martinez came toward them.

"Lindsey, Kelly will be fine." The petite Puerto Rican woman took both of Lindsey's hands and gave them a warm squeeze. "We set her leg. She's unconscious again, but we expect her to come around soon." She went on to explain that Kelly had broken both the tibia and fibula in her right leg, and that though she had a concussion, there was no skull fracture, hemorrhage or edema. "She woke up a couple of times while we worked on her leg. She'll be a bit disoriented for a little while and probably in and out of consciousness, but it's nature's way of healing, so don't be upset."

"When can I see her?"

"Here she comes now. We're taking her upstairs to a room, and you can stay with her for a while. It would be good for her to see you when she wakes up again. After that, I think you should get some rest and come back in the morning. We'll want to keep her here for about forty-eight hours."

A stretcher was rolled out, and Lindsey rushed to its side and caught her daughter's tiny hand. Kelly's lashes fluttered slightly and a faint smile flitted across her features, as if she knew her mother was nearby. Marcus quickly volunteered to call the ladies waiting in Baldridge while Lindsey accompanied her daughter to her room. She muttered her thanks again and entered the elevator with Kelly, Dr. Martinez and the attendants.

Once inside the hospital room, Lindsey stood by as her daughter was transferred to a bed, her plastered leg elevated slightly and then surrounded by ice packs to keep the swelling down. Dr. Martinez described how Lindsey should watch her daughter's toes for any sign of swelling or loss of circulation, and then quietly left the room.

Seated beside the bed, Lindsey gently stroked her daughter's small face and kissed her forehead. "Oh, Kelly, what have you done to yourself this time?" Settling back in the large wooden rocking chair provided, Lindsey rested her head on the high back but watched Kelly for any signs of returning consciousness. She wasn't aware that Marcus had entered until a large hand gently squeezed her shoulder.

"How's our girl?" His voice was quiet.

"She's still asleep, but she mutters now and then. How's everybody at home?" The words were out before she realized it. She sounded as if she were talking to a husband, not the man who had so flagrantly upset her equilibrium most of the day.

Marcus seemed not to notice as he pulled up a chair next to hers. "Everyone is of course relieved to hear that Kelly is going to be okay. I talked to Carrie, too. She told me to kiss her sister for her and her mommy." Before Lindsey realized what was happening, Marcus leaned toward her and kissed her on the lips, then straightened slightly to place a similar kiss on Kelly's cheek. As if his actions were completely commonplace, he settled back in his chair, one arm casually draped across the back of her rocker and one ankle propped on his other knee.

"Let me see. Mom and your grandmother told me to tell you that you're not to worry about anything at the house, and that they're keeping Carrie happy. Your grandmother is going to sleep in Kelly's bed tonight, in case Carrie gets lonesome." He paused and looked up at the ceiling squinting, his eyes closed, as if trying to remember a long list of messages. "Mom suggested that you use her room at my apartment while Kelly's in the hospital." He turned to a sputtering Lindsey and calmly pronounced, "That's about it."

"But—but I can't stay at your apartment. I . . ."

"No arguments, everything has been decided. Hmmm, there's something else. Oh, yes. Maggie made me promise that you would eat something." He checked his watch and announced, "It's almost eight now, and I don't know about you, but I'm getting hungry."

They sat for a while longer, hoping with each flutter of Kelly's long dark lashes that her eyes would open. Marcus suggested he try to find some sandwiches.

"Nothing for me, thank you. I'm really not hungry."

He placed one finger on her protesting lips and smiled. "No arguments. I have my orders. You're to eat something. I promised Maggie, remember?"

He was gone before she could offer any more arguments, leaving Lindsey to watch her daughter and bring some order to her scattered thoughts.

How had that man invaded her life so completely? She'd been in charge of herself and her household, and in less than twelve hours, Marcus Stafford had practically taken over. She was forced to admit in all honesty that she had been thankful for his presence during the long wait in the emergency room. He had relaxed her and kept her mind off all the terrible possibilities she would have imagined had she been alone.

She was still sorting out her thoughts when he returned, gleefully presenting two plastic-wrapped sandwiches and two cartons of milk. "You have your choice, milady. Ham and cheese or cheese and ham." He dropped one sandwich in her lap, accompanied by a napkin, and the carton of milk was thrust into her hand. "Eat! Or I'll be in *big* trouble." He plopped down in the chair he had vacated, unwrapped his bounty and took several bites. Quietly, he asked, "Any change?"

Lindsey toyed with her sandwich and took a few

sips of the cold milk. "Nothing." She forced herself to eat the food, washing the dry sandwich down with the milk while they both watched Kelly, periodically checking her toes as Dr. Martinez had instructed.

"Mommy?" Kelly's voice was so faint Lindsey thought she had imagined it. Then her daughter's lashes lifted, and she turned her head toward her. "Mommy?"

Lindsey jumped up to lean over the bed. "I'm here, darling. How do you feel?"

"My head hurts. And what's that thing on my leg?"

Smiling in joyful relief, Lindsey explained what had happened. "You'll get to stay in the hospital for another day or so, but I'll be here most of the time."

"Is Uncle Marcus here? I heard his voice." She searched the room until she spied him; then smiled broadly. "It's like having a real daddy, isn't it, Mommy?"

Glancing quickly toward Marcus and seeing his grin, Lindsey stammered, "Er . . . Marcus is . . . uh . . ."

"Hi, honey." Marcus interrupted her wild search for words. Standing beside her, he reached for one of Kelly's hands and gave it a little squeeze. "What was my best girl doing climbing up that ladder? You really scared your mommy and me."

Kelly frowned. "I'm sorry. I wasn't s'posed to be up there, was I."

"No, you weren't, young lady. But we're sure

glad you're going to be okay, now. Your mommy is awful tired. Can I take her home for a while?"

"Sure, if you kiss me good night," Kelly outrageously bargained. As she watched her daughter smile coyly up at Marcus, Lindsey wondered how anyone only four years old could be such a flirt.

"How could I resist anyone as beautiful as you?" Marcus leaned down and kissed Kelly on both cheeks and waited for a return of the favor and a hug from the delicate little arms that encircled his neck. The miniature temptress giggled when Marcus whispered something in her ear. "Now I want Mommy to kiss me before you put her to bed," she demanded.

Red-faced, Lindsey couldn't bear to look at Marcus as he stepped aside for her to wish her daughter a good night. Nor could she face him as he guided her out of the hospital to the waiting four-wheel-drive vehicle in the deserted parking lot. She promised herself she would find some way to gracefully eradicate the implications of permanence her daughter had made. She hoped he realized that four-year-olds, especially ones like Kelly, could suggest completely unreasonable and preposterous ideas.

She had to find a way to erase any misconceptions Marcus might have—as well as the tingling sensations she still felt on her lips from the light kiss he had bestowed beside her daughter's bed.

5

~∞∞∞∞∞∞∞∞∞∞∞~

Marcus gave Lindsey a gentle push as she reluctantly stepped forward into his apartment. While she stood uncertainly near the door, he walked ahead of her into a large living room and switched on a brass lamp. Lindsey gave a murmur of delight as the interior of his apartment became visible.

The first thing she saw was a huge skylight in the ceiling, a mirror of stars that shed a muted silver light on the plush dark brown velvet cushions of the modular furniture in the conversation pit. A modern free-standing fireplace separated the spacious living room from the kitchen, where she could see gleaming copper kettles and modern appliances. A thick cream-colored carpet covered the entire area, the three steps down to the center of the living room, then up to the edge of the kitchen where shiny rust-colored tile protected the floor.

When he switched on the recessed lighting in the kitchen, she couldn't believe her eyes. There was not a dish out of place. The airy space would have delighted the most exacting gourmet. Fresh herbs grew in small pots in a window greenhouse, baskets of vegetables and fruit hung from the ceiling above a wide butcher block, which contained several knife racks and wooden utensils stuffed in ceramic pots. Two stools stood before a gleaming formica bar, where a single place setting, consisting of heavy earthenware, ebony-handled cutlery and a tall glazed glass, lay in preparation for the next meal.

"I'm impressed," declared Lindsey, drawn to the kitchen by a sudden burst of insatiable curiosity. "Do you know how to use all the things in this kitchen?"

"I don't know how to use half of the stuff in here. A friend of mine is an interior decorator and I gave her carte blanche to furnish this place while I was away in Alaska last year. Her work here won an award."

Lindsey should have known he was involved with some woman. She wondered if his interior decorator had been given carte blanche in any other area of his life, then reminded herself that his personal affairs were none of her business. "Who takes care of the greenhouse when you're on one of your trips?" As soon as she heard the answer, Lindsey regretted asking.

"Bunny, across the hall, takes care of the plants. She's a gourmet cook, and her apartment is on the wrong side of the building to grow very much." Marcus shrugged. "She fixes me an occasional free meal in exchange for her use of my greenhouse."

Bunny? Lindsey envisioned a soft, fluffy creature who probably did a whole lot more than cook. She noticed how immaculately the apartment was kept, but didn't want to know who did the cleaning and didn't dare ask. He seemed to have a woman to fulfill every need. She wished she had the courage to ask him where she was supposed to fit in.

Of course! It came to her: she was the woman designated to take care of his widowed mother so he could get on with the Bunnys of the world. No wonder he was grateful to her for providing Vera with a happy home, far away from him and his harem.

Her paleness was taken by Marcus as a sign of her total exhaustion. Before she could ask him any more questions, he took her by the elbow and escorted her down the hall to the guest room.

"This is the room my mother uses when she visits. She lived here for a month or so after she sold the house." He switched on the light inside the spacious bedroom, showing Lindsey the evidence of Vera's feminine presence. The bed was covered by a crewel spread of delicate pink flowers scattered across a cream-colored field of natural linen. Matching drapes were tied back revealing light batiste sheers at the window.

Lindsey couldn't help but smile at the concessions Marcus had made in his masculine apartment for his very ladylike mother. His thoughtfulness and consideration constantly surprised her. She surveyed the marble-topped vanity, which was covered with a collection of perfume bottles, beribboned sachets and a large picture of Marcus. Without thinking, Lindsey stepped across the room and picked up the portrait to study it closer.

Marcus' laughing blue eyes stared back at her from the picture. But he had to have been years younger when it was taken, for his features were boyishly endearing, his physique not yet fully developed. Her intent concentration seemed to disturb him, for in the next second the ornate frame was taken out of her hands and the picture was abruptly replaced on the vanity.

"Me in my youth," he pronounced dismissively, then pointed to the doorway across the room. "That's the bathroom. You can have it first while I go make us something warm and soothing to drink. It'll help you sleep."

"And your room?" She couldn't help asking, aware of his nearness with every nerve and the intimacy of the apartment. Why had she agreed to come here? Why hadn't she remembered how he affected her?

She felt as if she were slowly emerging from a thick fog that had dulled all of her senses. She was just now becoming aware of the unsettling reality of her situation, which did nothing to soothe her already overwrought nerves. She was alone with Marcus, expected to sleep in the same apartment with him, and she had no real idea how it had come to pass.

Yes, she did! He had steamrolled her into accepting his offer of board, pointing out that Kelly would want her with her as soon as she woke up in the morning, that the women who waited at home in Baldridge wouldn't worry about her if they knew she were with him and that without transportation of her own she had little other choice than to rely on him. She had allowed him to escort her out of Kelly's room and out of the hospital, had meekly submitted to being hustled into his car and driven to his apartment. Now it was too late for second thoughts.

The frantic expression on her face must have been easily discernable, for Marcus was quick to reassure her that his intentions were honorable.

"My room's on the other side of the bathroom, but you can lock your door so you'll be assured of privacy. It may have looked otherwise this morning, Lindsey, but I don't take advantage of women when their defenses are down."

He looked straight into her eyes, willing her to read his sincerity. Her anxiety fled as swiftly as it had come.

"I believe you, Marcus," she whispered. "I . . . I . . ."

"You suddenly noticed that you were alone in a man's apartment." Marcus completed her sentence, turning away from her to walk toward the door. "Under the circumstances, I should probably take that as a compliment. After all that's happened today, it amazes me that you've found room for me in your thoughts at all, even if what you're thinking couldn't be farther from the truth. When Kelly's well again, we'll talk about that, but for now, just relax and stop worrying. Kelly's in good hands, and believe it or not, so are you."

She could hear his measured tread as he went down the hallway, stopped outside his bedroom, then went inside and closed the door behind him. Mechanically, feeling slightly ashamed of herself, Lindsey closed her door and leaned weakly back against the smooth wood. Admonishing herself that she was being ridiculous, that they were both mature adults, she concentrated on her surroundings.

Suddenly it dawned on her that she had brought nothing with her to wear for the night—didn't even have a toothbrush! She whirled around and re-opened the door, intending to ask her host if he could lend her something to sleep in, but Marcus was a step ahead of her. She literally walked right into him in the hall. His large hands settled on her shoulders until she regained her balance and was able to take a shaky step backwards.

"Don't panic." His amused tone brought swift color to her cheeks. "My pajama top and this robe should cover you from top to bottom."

"Thank you," she managed as he thrust the clothing into her arms.

She knew she was staring up at him as if he were some kind of fearsome apparition that had materialized right in front of her eyes, but she couldn't help it. He was so male, and she had never felt smaller or more vulnerable in her life. As if caught in some hypnotic trance, she stood perfectly still, until a muscle leaped along his jaw and again he turned away from her.

"I'll give you twenty minutes, then I'm coming into your room with that drink I promised," he muttered grimly, then strode back down the hallway toward the kitchen. She stood staring after him until she heard the loud slam of a cupboard door, followed by the resounding clatter of a pan being placed none too gently on the burner of the stove. Her behavior had both angered and offended him, and he seemed to be taking his feelings out on the inanimate objects in his kitchen.

For some reason, the sound of him angrily slamming doors and muttering loudly under his breath lent her courage. She had often taken her frustrations and temper out on the unfeeling utensils of her own kitchen, slamming doors and jerking pots and pans off the shelves as if they were guilty of causing her problems. She and Marcus seemed to have something in common, if only the habit of manhandling kitchenware.

"I love cocoa," she raised her voice loud enough to reach him. Immediately, all was silent from the kitchen.

But as Lindsey turned back to the bedroom, she could hear Marcus whistling some off-key tune that seemed to sound, at least to her, both gratified and slightly apologetic. She smiled and closed the bedroom door behind her, feeling gratified and slightly apologetic herself.

Exactly twenty minutes later, Marcus knocked on the door to her bedroom. Lindsey sat propped up against the lace-edged pillows, her hair spread like a veil across her shoulders, wearing the top of his pajamas, which reached well below her knees. She had had to roll up the sleeves a half dozen times in order to find her wrists and refused to make matters worse by putting on the all-enveloping terry robe he had given her. It was a warm night in June, and although Marcus' apartment was air conditioned, she had no need for a heavy robe. For modesty's sake, she slid her legs beneath the sheet and gave him permission to enter, hoping she could stay awake long enough to accept his hospitable offer for a soothing drink.

"Good girl." He gave her an approving smile. "Now you can drink this and go right to sleep. You've had a rough day."

"What is it?" Lindsey, who had been expecting a mug of hot chocolate, eyed the tall glass in his hand suspiciously. She hid her reaction to the sight of him, his hair still damp from the shower she had heard him take, the short maroon robe that barely covered his knees. Was he wearing anything beneath it? It couldn't be much, for when he sat down on the mattress beside her and held out the glass of white liquid, she got a disturbing glimpse of a bare, hair-roughened thigh.

"Warm milk and honey." Marcus was unaware

of her breathless reaction to his scanty attire, thinking her slow acceptance of his offered beverage was due to fatigue.

"I thought I was going to get cocoa." She took the glass, keeping her eyes downcast so he wouldn't see her awareness of him in them.

"My mother swears by hot milk, but I always add a dash of honey to sweeten the taste. Drink it down and you'll sleep like a baby."

She took a tentative sip—anything to hasten his departure from the room. Her eyes had a willful tendency to stray to the gap in his robe and the slight show of skin that was visible.

The drink wasn't bad tasting and she gulped it down quickly, running her tongue over her lips to erase the last remnants of milk. When she handed back the glass she found that he was staring at her mouth, seemingly fascinated. It was as if a static current had suddenly been switched on inside him.

Lindsey stared back at him, equally fascinated by his reaction to her. His blue eyes were liquid sky, his mouth held a sensual twist as his face suffused with dark color and he began to breathe as if he had been running.

"Sleep well." He was off the bed in a quick economy of movement and striding just as quickly to the door. Once there, he turned back, as if unable to stop himself and uttered, self-derisively, "If you need anything, I'll—I mean . . . Oh, hell, Lindsey, this wasn't such a great idea after all. Good night." As he had done earlier in the kitchen, he took out his feelings by slamming her door.

Lindsey's brown eyes grew wide, wider as she comprehended his behavior. He wanted her! It had been years since she'd felt the breathtaking surge of feminine power that exists in every woman who knows she has made a man desire her. It was an extremely heady sensation and one that, instead of making her nervous and upset, made her feel as if something that had been lacking in her life for far too long a time had just been given back to her. A very handsome man wanted her so badly that he had behaved quite out of character!

Marcus Stafford was an outrageous flirt who enjoyed teasing women, and was sure of himself with the opposite sex, but the man who had slammed out of her room tonight had not been teasing and hadn't looked very sure of his ability to stay in control of himself. Lindsey hugged the knowledge to herself like a precious gem, then offered a prayer for the continued safety of her young daughter and closed her eyes to sleep, a beatific smile curving her lips.

Lindsey stood paralyzed, watching in horror, as Kelly fell from the towering ladder that reached upward to infinity. "Mommy! Mommy!" Her pitiful screams tore at Lindsey's heart but she couldn't reach her, couldn't break her fall into the black abyss that opened beneath her falling body.

"Kelly!" Lindsey screamed, tears flowing down her cheeks as the dark head disappeared into the depths and her terrified calls receded into oblivion. "No! No! God, please—please!"

"Hush now, sweetheart." Strong arms captured Lindsey and drew her away from the murky cavern where her child lay in a crushed heap. She fought the restraining arms, screaming that she had to reach Kelly, help her, until the deep male voice brought her back to reality with a sharp jolt. "Lindsey, wake up! You're dreaming. It's only a dream."

Sobbing and shaking with terror, Lindsey clung to the hard body that held her. She couldn't think coherently, the images of her daughter in the nightmare too vividly fresh in her mind. "I couldn't move, couldn't reach her," she babbled hysterically.

Marcus lifted her onto his lap as if she were a child, rocking her sobbing body and murmuring words of comfort into her hair. "It's okay. Kelly's safe, Lindy."

Lindsey didn't know how much time had elapsed before she realized who was holding her and that she was no longer seeking comfort from him, but was reveling in the feel of his hard, warm body against hers, enjoying the touch of his blunt fingers massaging her neck. Slowly, she became aware that her head was resting upon the smooth, naked flesh of his chest. His skin felt warm and moist beneath her cheek. One of her hands was clutched in a fist over his heart, and she gradually unfolded her fingers and felt the steady beat. She trembled from a shaft of awareness as the center of her sensitive palm was pricked by a hardened male nipple. Her involuntary shiver brought another husky endearment. "You're safe, angel."

His tone was oddly choked, and Lindsey heard him utter a soft groan as she adjusted herself upon his legs, unconsciously sliding her hand around his waist, her fingertips brushing along the elastic band of his pale blue boxer shorts. She couldn't help herself but snuggled against him, tilting her head in order to look up at his face. Didn't he know that she wanted him to kiss her? She could feel his hardened desire, but sensed that he was holding himself in tight check. His expression was pained, his stubborn chin held tautly, his blue eyes almost black, the mischievous dimples in his cheeks nonexistent. His gleaming hair, silvered in the moonlight, fell across his forehead. Lindsey's lips parted in awe over his stark male beauty. She took a deep breath and inhaled his scent, a brisk tangy aroma like the freshest ocean breeze. "Marcus?" she whispered, her longing reflected in the smoldering shadows of her dark eyes.

"Oh, God, Lindsey." He groaned and enslaved her lips with his hungry mouth. Her soft tongue glided tentatively between his lips and whetted his appetite even further until he slid her body from his lap and pressed her down upon the mattress. Supporting himself on one arm, he looked down at her face, as if to convince himself that she was willing. Then, seeing the glowing invitation in her thickly lashed eyes, he lowered himself over her and resumed their kiss.

Within moments, he had unbuttoned her pajama top and his fingers began a tactile exploration that was both tender and exciting. Lindsey sucked in her breath as he palmed her small breast, pressing her nipple between two of his fingers as he gathered her feminine softness into his large hand. She couldn't resist him, didn't want to do anything but use her hands to memorize him. Every rib and smooth muscle, every disk of the straight spine, the virile muscles of his buttocks pressed tight beneath his thin cotton shorts, his powerful thighs. She made soft sounds of delight with each new discovery, arching herself against him in mindless wonder. She had never felt more alive, alive and loving— being loved. She threaded her hands through the silky gold of his hair and trembled with delirious joy as his mouth opened over one nipple, complimenting its texture with his tongue as he satisfied the yearning that became a crescendo inside her.

"Oh, Marcus," she moaned with sweet longing. But instead of inspiring him to continue his molten exploration, her words brought an immediate stiffening to his spine. Seconds later, her heated flesh was chilled by the cool air around them as Marcus lifted himself away from her to sit up on the edge of the bed. He covered his face with both hands, breathed deeply until he had regained some semblance of control, then stood up and drew the sheet over her shivering body.

"Don't look at me like that." He passed one hand over his forehead. "I can't take you like this, Lindsey. It wouldn't be fair. You've been through so much today that if I made love to you, I would never know if you'd given yourself to me because you were vulnerable or because you really wanted me the way I want you. When we do make love, you'll be fully aware of what you're doing. And then, I'll take everything you have to give without a qualm."

She was too shocked to say anything, amazed that he could bring himself to an abrupt halt in the midst of their turbulent lovemaking when she knew it would have been impossible for her to ask him to stop. Was he right? Did she only want him tonight to make her feel secure? To block out the horror of her nightmare? Had she melted under his touch because she wanted a man to comfort her, to make love to her? Was she only using him because she needed to be cared for? No, that wasn't what had made her desire him more than any man she'd ever known, even more than she had desired Peter.

She had wanted him to make love to her because she loved everything about him. His kindness, his humor, the approval in his eyes whenever he looked at her. If she didn't think love at first sight was an impossibility, she might believe that she had actually fallen in love with the man. But she was too practical to put any faith in that notion.

As the passion drained away from her, it was replaced by a numbing exhaustion that sapped her strength and made her want to cry.

"You're very kind, Marcus." She knew she had to say something and could think of nothing else.

"Kind?" He cleared his throat and turned his

back on her, walking quickly to the door. "Not kind, Lindsey Delaney. My plans for you are quite selfish and thoroughly greedy. I wouldn't call them kind, not in a million years."

Seeing the confused and tearful expression on her face, the shudders of her petite body, he shook his head and swore softly under his breath before returning to the side of the bed. With the efficiency of an unfeeling automaton, Marcus lifted the discarded top of his pajamas off the sheets and began to re-dress her. He buttoned every button, then took a firm hold on her shoulders and pressed her down onto the mattress. He drew the covers over her, tucking them in beneath her as she sometimes did with her children when they were suffering from a cold and couldn't get warm. He left her side only long enough to go to the closet and pull out a blanket, shaking it out and laying it over her.

"Now you're treating me as if I were a child like Kelly or Carrie. I'm perfectly capable of taking care of myself, Marcus Stafford, and I don't need you to tuck me in." She couldn't keep up with his change of moods. One minute he was teasing and devil-may-care, the next he was all passionate, demanding lover, and then he became almost paternally solicitous and tender. His ability to change gears so completely annoyed her and she was so tired, her lower lip began to quiver exactly as if she were one of the children she had resolutely declared she was not.

"All of us need someone to take care of us once in a while, angel." He bent over and gave her an affectionate kiss on one cheek. "You take care of other people every day of your life, so don't begrudge yourself a little tender loving care for a change. Besides, I'm determined to give it to you, whether you want me to or not."

She was too tired to be irritated, her heavy lashes falling down over her pale cheeks no matter how hard she tried to prevent it. "Do you always get what you want, Marcus?" she whispered softly as fatigue claimed her completely and she fell into a deep sleep.

"Not always, but where you're concerned, I intend to."

Lindsey didn't hear his answer or see the determined glint that came into his blue eyes as he stood staring down at her sleeping form. He returned to his own room only when he had gazed his full at each feature.

6

〜〜〜〜〜〜〜〜〜

Mommy!" Kelly called as soon as she spied her mother. When she saw who was accompanying Lindsey into the hospital room, her smile widened and her eyes became more animated. "Uncle Marcus."

"Good morning, sweetheart." Lindsey crossed the room and enclosed her daughter in her arms, accepting Kelly's enthusiastic bear hug and resounding kiss. After releasing her, she stepped back and was not surprised when Kelly greeted Marcus in a similar fashion. Her happiness at seeing her daughter alert, cheerful and sitting propped up on the bed was marred only by the increasing discomfort she felt over Kelly's growing affection for Marcus.

The tall man was regaling Kelly with rapid-fire jokes only a four-year-old would appreciate. Kelly was enthralled with him, but he could step out of their lives as quickly as he had stepped in. How would Kelly deal with that? And how would Lindsey be able to explain it to her? Kelly was openly affectionate with most people, but her relationship with Marcus had already progressed beyond that. Lindsey feared the little girl would be crushed when he was no longer around to play at being surrogate father. It was obvious that the twins yearned for a daddy, and to them, Marcus was the perfect choice. That he nonchalantly accepted the role they had cast him in, openly returning their affection, seemed to Lindsey almost cruel. How could he lead them on so? He appeared to be highly content with his present life-style, and Lindsey doubted that a ready-made family would fit into his future plans. By his own admission, he had several women in his life—enough to fill every need. His free-wheeling, come-and-go habits negated both permanency and monogamy.

Lindsey realized they would see him occasionally as long as Vera lived with them, but if the past months were any indication, those visits would be infrequent and she did not approve of the familial attachment he was implying with her children. She had been taught to address blood relatives as "aunt" or "uncle" and the twins' usage of the term "uncle" for Marcus offended her sense of propriety. She would have to find a way to explain to the children that Marcus would be only a sporadic visitor, not a member of their extended family, no matter how much they might wish he would be.

In the clear light of day, Lindsey had viewed the events of the previous night more objectively. She knew that if she weren't careful, she would be as naively drawn to Marcus as the twins were. His manner during breakfast and the short drive to the hospital had given her no indication that he felt more for her than friendship—as if the moments in his arms the night before had never been. There had been none of the sexual tension that had been so strong between them the night before, when she had nearly asked him to make love to her.

Remembering the way she had reacted to his touch, she blushed. Peter had been the only man she had ever gone to bed with, and not until after their marriage. Last night, it had been Marcus, not her, who had pulled away, telling her he wanted her, but not when she was so emotionally vulnerable. She supposed that she should have been grateful he had not taken advantage of her, knowing as she did now that last night he had been showing nothing but humane concern for a distraught woman. His brusque manner this morning was a clear indication that he regretted his actions of the previous night.

She listened as Kelly gave Marcus a long list of messages for everyone at home, and smiled when Kelly asked him to bring her favorite doll back with him. While Lindsey continued to nervously muse about the previous night, he had been explaining that he was going to spend the day in Baldridge and wouldn't be returning until late afternoon.

"I'll remember to bring Georgie. Is there anything else you want, princess?" His rich voice was soft, and the little girl looked up at him with adoring eyes.

"No, that's all. 'Cept, bring you back to see me." Kelly's dark silky hair fell away from her face as she stretched out her arms, inviting him to hug her before he left. Marcus' light blond hair was in sharp contrast to the dark curls that fell against it as Kelly received her good-bye hug and his promise to return. After Lindsey gave him her own list of necessities to bring from home, he quickly left.

With Marcus gone, the hospital room suddenly seemed cold and sterile. She felt a strange sense of loss. Her hand still tingled from the quick squeeze he had given her fingers when he had passed by her on his way out. She was brought back to reality by Kelly's chatter about hospital routine. The little girl was delighted with the attention she was getting and happily described the treat that had been brought to her on her breakfast tray.

Later in the morning, Dr. Martinez arrived to check Kelly's progress.

"There's been no abnormal swelling in her leg, and since she's her usual cheery self, I don't think we need worry about complications."

That prognosis was the most wonderful pronouncement Lindsey could have heard. She was further reassured as the small, dark-haired physician went on to say there was no reason Kelly couldn't be released the next day. Lindsey was grateful to learn that keeping Kelly another night was only being undertaken as a precautionary measure.

Although Lindsey was ecstatic with the news, the small pixie propped up against the gaily printed pillows appeared disappointed. It was obvious that Kelly was enjoying her "special care" at the hospital, and Lindsey made a mental note to herself. She didn't want Kelly spoiled by all the extra attention she would be receiving for the next few weeks and knew if she didn't take prompt action, Kelly could easily turn into a prima donna of the worst sort. She could just imagine the strong-minded child having everyone in the household jumping at a snap of her tiny fingers.

By late afternoon, Lindsey's voice was hoarse from all the story-telling and reading she had done by Kelly's bedside. The little invalid's avid interest in the family of ducklings marching through a Boston park was unending—until Marcus breezed into the room, laden with treasures from home, most especially the very battered, long-suffering rag doll, Georgie. In one hand he dangled a wicker basket that was brimming with gaily wrapped packages.

"It's like Christmas!" Kelly exclaimed over the small presents each member of the family had sent. While Kelly's attention was diverted, Marcus turned to greet Lindsey.

"How about you, Mommy? Did you have a good day?" His blue eyes danced with merriment as he held her gaze. Lindsey fought down the urge to hope, like Kelly, that Marcus might one day become a permanent member of their family. Why did he have to call her "mommy" in such a natural way, as if he might be the "daddy"?

"I . . . It was fine. Dr. Ann says that Kelly can go home tomorrow." She couldn't resist answering his smile. The man was a Pied Piper around women. The young and the old, none could resist him. "Did you finish the roof?" It was the only thing she could think of to say, and she could have kicked herself. After all he had done for her and her family, she had to ask if he had completed his original task. She had sounded like some harsh taskmaster, unconcerned with anything but the work needing to be done on her house.

His biting tone told her exactly how he felt about her ungrateful question. "Matter of fact, I did." When he saw her stricken expression, he relented and made his tone light. "I managed to repair a few other things, too. It's a charming old house with a lot of charming little things broken. I just may have to spend my whole vacation getting everything squared away."

"Thank you for all you've done." Lindsey was sure he didn't want to spend his time off from work fixing up an old house. "I can't let you do more than you've already done."

"I'm volunteering." He flashed a wide grin. "I enjoy fixing things, but I seldom get the chance." He followed his announcement with a complete inspection of her with his eyes, dimpling boyishly and tilting his head to one side. "Would you deny me one of *my* life's greatest pleasures?"

"Uncle Marcus," Kelly cried breathlessly, clasping to her chest a beautifully illustrated picture book by Tasha Tudor. "I love it. Thank you, thank you."

Marcus' gaze swung to Kelly and he immediately walked over and sat down on the edge of her bed. "You're very welcome. Grandma Vera told me that you love fairy tales, and this book is full of stories about princesses just like you."

Grandma Vera? What was he doing? The girls had always called Vera by her first name, and now suddenly they had not only acquired a new "uncle" but an additional "grandmother" as well. The children loved Vera and the other women as much as if they had been their real grandmothers, but that title was reserved for Althea. He was going too far—setting up false hopes in her daughters' minds. She was determined to put a stop to it.

Kelly chattered on and on while Marcus managed to make the appropriate responses. He was even able to insert enough of his own in the conversation to make Kelly giggle helplessly from time to time.

As Lindsey watched them together, her resolution to speak with him became a matter of extreme importance. She wanted to yell at him to stop being so sweet to her daughter, yet didn't have the courage to utter a word.

"I think you can do without your mommy until tomorrow morning, don't you, princess?" Marcus asked and received Kelly's affirmative nod. He turned a devastating smile on Lindsey, then announced, "I'm under orders to make you eat properly. What do you say about going out for a nice dinner?"

"That's impossible." Lindsey was hard pressed to withstand his smile. "I've nothing with me but this sundress. I'll get something in the coffee shop. I—I—"

A firm finger pressed over her parted lips stopped further argument but started her pulse racing at top speed. While Marcus looked deeply into her dark eyes, his long blunt forefinger lingered to delicately outline the contours of her mouth. "No arguments, remember?" His voice was the final inducement against her, low and husky like sandpaper across velvet. "Althea packed a bag for you and assured me you'd have something appropriate to wear. Lindey's restaurant isn't far from my apartment, so we can walk over there. It'll do you good to get out and enjoy the beautiful weather we're having."

Mesmerized by the warm invitation that had nothing to do with the weather, Lindsey accepted, and after a whirlwind exchange of hugs and kisses with her daughter, they left Kelly's room.

Marcus hustled her down the corridor and out of the hospital, his large hand never leaving the small of her back as he propelled her along. She gained the impression he was afraid she might change her mind, and tried not to laugh when he swiftly dusted off the vinyl covers inside his rather battered looking jeep so she wouldn't soil her dress, then did laugh when he hopped into the car and swerved out of the parking lot. Ten minutes later, he was ushering her into his apartment. He handed her a small overnight case and a garment bag, then promptly informed her that she could use the shower first.

Following his firm command, Lindsey was soon standing beneath the warm water spraying steadily from the shower head in his luxurious bathroom. She had barely acknowledged, prior to this, that the room contained far more than standard equipment. As she stepped out of the shower, she took note of the artfully decorated room. It was a showplace! The glass-encased shower stall stood in one corner. Across from it was a mirrored wall with a long counter containing two sinks. Most impressive of all was the raised round whirlpool centered in the room. Glancing longingly toward it, she dried herself with one of the chocolate-colored bath sheets stacked on an enameled bench. A soft pink light warmed her skin, and she glanced up at the recessed heat lamp in the ceiling. How could she have missed all of this, last night and this morning, she asked herself. *I must have been in some kind of stupor!* If Marcus hadn't been waiting to use the bathroom, she would have loved to luxuriate in the bubbling water of his private spa. That thought was swiftly followed by a disturbing image of him joining her beneath the bubbles, and she briskly brought those kind of images to an end by making an outrageous face at herself in the mirror.

Wrapped in yards of the thick terry cloth, she

opened her bedroom door and called out to Marcus, "It's all yours."

Inside the guest room, she crossed to the garment bag hanging on the closet door. What did you choose for me, Grandma? she silently asked as she unzipped the bag. She was momentarily surprised when she removed the whimsically romantic dress she had bought last summer in one of her rare moods of extravagance. Oh, dear, you're being so obvious! she chided her grandmother, then said out loud, "I should have called home myself and specified what I wanted."

Searching through the overnight case, she found the appropriate accessories, fresh underwear and a casual slack ensemble. The garment bag had yielded nothing more than a tailored cotton shirtwaist, not at all fitting for an evening at one of the city's chic bistros. She had no other choice, then, but to slip into the soft turquoise and white organza, whose flowing skirt swirled around her knees. She adjusted the fragile spaghetti straps and fluffed the ruffle that fell across her bosom, viewing herself in the mirror. Her long, thick hair hung casually over one shoulder in a style she found immature. Rummaging through her case, she found her curling iron and an assortment of combs, brushes and pins. Ruefully acknowledging her reasons for wanting to look like a mature woman, she swept her hair back from her face and secured it with ivorylike combs. She curled the loose tendrils and was pleased with the flattering result. When she was done with her hair, she slipped her sheer-hosed feet into strappy-heeled sandals, then whirled in a graceful circle. How long had it been since she had truly looked forward to going out with someone? Her thoughts drifted to Marcus, but at the sound of him leaving the bathroom, she went swiftly to the vanity to apply her makeup.

Finding her unopened bottle of perfume amongst her other toiletries, she applied a small amount of the breezy floral cologne to her wrists and throat. Why not? My grandmother and his mother must have spent an entire afternoon gathering these seductive props. She smiled to herself and fastened small ivory hoops in her ears. After a quick assessing glance in the mirror, she picked up her small white bag and draped a fringed silk shawl over her arm. Under her breath, she muttered, "Neither one of us stands a chance with this army of matchmakers." Then she walked out into the hallway.

Marcus was waiting for her in the living room. He turned at the sound of her footsteps, and emitted a long, low wolf whistle through his teeth. "I'm not sure it's safe to walk even a few blocks with you." His cerulean eyes complimented the feminine vision floating toward him. "Maybe I should carry a weapon to fend off your admirers," he teased. He took the shawl from her arm and dropped it over her shoulders. His hands remained where they were overlong, and she didn't dare breathe or move. "Mmmm, you smell wonderful. Like you rolled in a garden of all the flowers in the world."

She was becoming addicted to his flamboyant compliments and had to remember that they came far too easily to his lips. A breathtaking tingle coursed down her spine as he bent his head and nuzzled the curve at the base of her neck. "We'd better go, or I'll have you for dinner."

Reluctantly, he released her and stepped to one side so he could read the expression on her face. It appeared to satisfy him, for he dropped an approving kiss on the tip of her nose and gallantly extended his arm. "Come, you beautiful thing. I'll do my best to keep back the poor men who'll be on our trail from here to the restaurant."

Falling in with his playful mood and irresistible smile, Lindsey laughed. "You're ridiculous!" She slipped her arm through his, then returned his appraisal. "You look pretty good yourself—that is for a 'worker-man.'"

"Yeah, we 'worker-men' look all right when we clean up," he jested, agreeably mimicking the twins' terminology.

They certainly do, Lindsey thought to herself as she walked with him out of the apartment building and onto the brick sidewalk. He had changed into a tropical-weight suit. The dark muted plaid was combined with a crisp cotton shirt of ecru and a conservative tie. She recognized the tangy fragrance he wore, and it subtly beckoned to her, making her want to lean closer and breathe more deeply of the elusive scent. Giggling softly, she admitted that they both looked good and smelled good; their sponsors would have been proud of them. The stage was set, and she might as well enjoy it for the short time it lasted. Later she could disentangle herself from the transparent web their relatives had spun to ensnare them.

The twilight sun setting in the summer sky cast enough light for Lindsey to visually enjoy the stroll through picturesque German Village. Not many years ago, she knew the area had been one of the capital city's worst slum districts and been designated for leveling by an urban renewal program. Several concerned citizens had formed a group to save the area, and the restoration of the small red brick dwellings had begun. Property values had since soared, and today, with a large part of the village restored, it had become one of the most sought-after living areas for singles and young marrieds. The annual "Haus and Garten" show was always popular and encouraged the residents to continue their beautification efforts. The German flavor of the area was particularly enhanced by the many window boxes spilling over with brightly colored flowers and the wrought-iron gates that enclosed the brilliant displays in beautifully land-scaped courtyards. They paused along the way to peer into the store windows of the varied specialty shops located in the area, and Lindsey was surprised at the number of times they would each point out and admire the same article.

She was enjoying herself and had to admit that Marcus had been right. She had needed to get outside and away from the stifling atmosphere inside the hospital. German Village was located in the center of a modern metropolitan city, the home of more than a million people, but there was a charming Old World quality about it that came as a refreshing breath of air. They entered the French setting of Lindey's, passed by the copper-topped bar and were ushered to a table on the second floor. They chatted desultorily, appreciating the distant sound of music played by the jazz trio on the first floor as they enjoyed their before-dinner drinks.

Although the alcoholic beverage would normally have helped to relax her, Lindsey found herself becoming more and more tense as she began receiving the nonverbal messages being sent to her by her dinner companion. By the time the waiter arrived to take their order, she was incapable of protesting as Marcus high-handedly ordered the house specialty, sautéed tournedos with Béarnaise sauce, for them both. Every lazily drawled word he uttered seemed like a caress, every glance an open invitation to join him in a far more intimate activity than dinner.

"I chose this place because of you." He leisurely appraised the high color in her cheeks and edged his chair closer. "Lindey has become a name I enjoy hearing again and again. I suppose I'll be forced to dine here all of the time if I can't get a better invitation elsewhere."

Lindsey chose to ignore the last part of his sentence and concentrated instead on the initial compliment. "Thank you, but I'm not letting that remark go to my head. You are such a flirt, Marcus.

Tell me, how does a woman know when you are being sincere and when you are merely trying to charm your way into her—'' Appalled, she bit back what she was about to say, hoping he'd have the decency not to ask her to complete her sentence.

"If I'm attempting to charm a woman into my bed, I'm always sincere." He looked amused, then frowned. "Why do I get the impression you think there's a revolving door in my bedroom?"

Lindsey cleared her throat nervously, took a sip of the wine Marcus had ordered, then attempted an answer. "I can't picture you without female companionship, Marcus. You're just not the type."

A guarded expression came into his eyes, but he didn't pursue the subject. Lindsey was grateful that their food arrived and she could concentrate on making a good show of enjoying the meal. The sensation that he was steadily moving closer to her was not wholly in her mind, for when coffee was poured after dinner, his chair was right next to hers. His thigh occasionally brushed against hers, continually building the sexual awareness between them. She had planned to deliver a stern lecture tonight, tell him not to foster any more false paternal dreams in her children, but he was constantly throwing her off guard and sidetracking her train of thought. If he wasn't smiling at her as if she were the most interesting woman on earth, he was speaking about the twins, and like mothers everywhere, she absorbed every word of his earnest praise without interruption.

"By the way," he enthused, "I managed to fix

that old chair lift by the stairs. With all that plaster on Kelly's leg, she'll probably weigh twice as much as usual when we bring her home. Now it will be much easier for us to get her up and down those stairs."

Us? We? Lindsey was about to burst into the pointed speech she had prepared when again she got diverted.

"You should've seen Carrie riding up and down that thing all afternoon." Marcus laughed. "The little pixie had me running up and down those stairs beside her while she rode like a queen seated on an electric throne."

Lindsey couldn't help laughing as he swiftly launched into a full-scale description of Carrie's enraptured expression. "I can see those big blue eyes of hers as round as saucers."

She was unaware of his small sigh of relief. She assumed his raised brow was his way of showing total interest in their conversation; actually, he was congratulating himself for detouring her from expressing her disapproval with him for including himself in the references made about her and her family. Luckily, she didn't know that her feelings on that subject were easily read—and, he hoped, just as easily changed.

"That was a very thoughtful thing to do." Lindsey was happy to stay on the safe topic he had begun. "Your mother and the other women can use the lift, too. So many accidents take place on the stairs, and now I won't have to worry about that happening."

"Perhaps you should worry less about everyone else and more about yourself," Marcus remarked, lifting her hand and curling his fingers around it. "Of course, now that you're in my hands . . ." The suggestive tone of his voice made her distinctly uncomfortable, and she snatched her hand away, keeping it out of reach beneath the table.

She laughed to cover her nervousness. "I don't need a man to protect me, Marcus. I'm a full-grown woman who has been on her own for several years."

"Not any more." The honeyed voice coated her with tenderness.

Her gaze swept to his face, but she found none of the indulgent mockery that could usually be seen in his eyes. Once she looked at him, she was unable to look away, and the longer she looked, the more enchanted she became. He was a sorcerer, using twin points of blue magic to cast his spell upon her, fascinate her. When he added the male wizardry of his husky low voice, she was spellbound.

"Be with me, Lindy?" Both a question and a plea that she couldn't answer in any way but by nodding her head. "Then let's get out of here before I make a slathering fool out of myself in public."

That made her laugh, breaking the tension between them. But he quickly brought it back to an intense level.

"You should laugh more often," he breathed softly. "It's like music."

She felt the caress of his ultramarine eyes

through every pore and was quite willing when, without another word, he stood up and helped her from her chair. With single-minded purpose, he paid the bill, placed her shawl over her shoulders and led her out of the restaurant and onto the street.

He kept one arm possessively around her as they strolled together down the night-darkened cobbled sidewalk. The warm glow from the glass-enclosed streetlights was nothing compared to the leaping flames mounting to an inferno inside her with each step they took closer to his apartment. Every nerve in her body was on fire. The brush of his thigh against her as they walked made her reel until she slid one arm around his waist to maintain her balance. He immediately tightened his grip and bent his head to whisper harshly in her ear. "Tonight is ours, Lindy. Yours and mine alone."

The air was heavy with gathering dew and the heady perfume of flowers, but she was oblivious to anything and everything but the man beside her.

"Ours alone," she promised softly in return, the light tapping of her heels on the bricks the only sound in the night-hushed shadows. She felt as if she were floating, and leaned closer to him as they approached his apartment building. The undeniable magnetism connecting them, the romantic atmosphere surrounding them, combined to wash away all her reservations and she succumbed to his powerful brand of enticement, relegating a fleeting second thought to the back of her mind.

He unlocked the door and she preceded him into

the darkened living room. She took only a few steps before he pulled her into his arms.

"Lindsey," he whispered, then lowered his head and crushed her lips beneath his. She melted into him, heady with the sensual delight of his assaulting tongue tantalizing the interior of her mouth. Her arms wound around his shoulders and her fingers winnowed through the thick golden hair at the back of his head. Her shawl slithered from her shoulders, falling silently to the floor, and Marcus smoothed his fingertips along her bare skin, finally unzipping her dress to expose her back to his questing touch. His kiss deepened as he splayed his large hands across her back, then moved it lower to cup her firm, rounded buttocks and bring her lower body into close contact with the tangible evidence of his desire.

Breathless from their long kiss Lindsey moaned faintly beneath his mouth until he moved his lips across her cheek and down her neck. She arched against him, gasping with pleasure when his lips skimmed along her shoulders. Her dress quickly joined her shawl on the floor as he tenderly pulled her hands from him and lowered them down to her sides. She clung to him tightly when he lifted her into his arms and his mouth engulfed hers. He carried her the few yards to the conversation pit and laid her on the large velvet-covered cushions. Stepping back, he removed his jacket and tie and loosened the tails of his shirt, unbuttoning it as he returned to her side. In a desire-laden trance, Lindsey reached for him and slid the shirt away from his wide, squared shoulders, basking in the heated depths of his darkened eyes as he leaned over her.

"Oh, God, I want you Lindsey—even if it's still not the best time. I went crazy last night after I left you." He lowered himself over her, his chest barely touching hers, the soft body hair that clouded his heavily muscled torso grazed her breasts with sensual delight as her nipples hardened to peaks. One of his hands moved between their bodies, his palm covering one breast, then drifting to the other, where his fingertips encircled the rosy aureole. She squirmed beneath him, her hands running over his long, broad back, loving the primeval maleness of him.

As one hand continued a soaring arousal of her breasts, his other slid her remaining garments from her. He rolled away only long enough to rid himself of his own clothing, then joined her amongst the cushions, lying on his side, propping his head in one hand while the other cupped her face. He kissed her leisurely, drugging her. She rolled onto her side to bring herself into full contact with him, but his hand at her shoulder arrested her. "No, I want to look at you," he said hoarsely. "You're so beautiful, so perfect." He ran his hand down her body from her neck across her breast to her stomach. The room was dimly lit by the large skylight directly overhead where a cloudless sky, sparkling with stars and a crescent moon, shone silvered light down upon her slim ivory body. He traced the thready white scars that had resulted from her pregnancy, and Lindsey retreated from his exploring fingertips. "Don't," he growled. "Those mark the woman you are. They're a part of you, and I want to know all of you." His voice was shaky as he took her hand and guided it to his chest. "Know me, Lindsey, all of me."

Lindsey's fingertips and eyes swept across his chest and down his torso. Muscles beneath the warm, moist surfaces leaped in response to her touch, and she was aware for the first time of her own sensual power over a man. Never in her married life had she experienced anything like this. His breathing grew rapid and heavy as she continued her exploration. He matched her touch for touch until they gradually intensified to ardent tormenting caresses that scattered rapidly across their bodies. Driven by a mindless need for release from the overpowering tension, she pressed against him, yearning for the feel of his bold maleness within her soft flesh, and was swept beneath. He fit his body between her thighs and his mouth descended on hers, parting her lips easily with the probing insistence of his tongue.

She moaned in shameless pleasure, fitting herself more closely against him as she responded to the hungry demand of his exploring hands and tongue. His heated skin slid down her body, and his mouth left hers to begin a seemingly endless journey down her throat and across her breasts. The small concentric circles he drew with his tongue around her hardened, throbbing nipples set off depth charges of delight that became more and more intense as his fingers traced lower and his lips followed the sensitized fuse they had laid along her skin.

His tender caresses of the core of her sensuality were both searingly intimate and exquisitely gentle. She thought she might faint from ecstasy, but he proved she was capable of enduring far more potent endearments. The infinitely sweet agony of his stroking tongue went on and on until his warm breath trailed flame along her inner thighs, over her stomach, then back up between her breasts. She grasped hold of his taut buttocks, as he came to her, then set a rocking rhythm within her that she matched with wanton eagerness. The surging male power of him filled her and thrust her even higher and higher until she blazed in the wondrous explosion they each set off in the other.

"Marcus . . . Marcus," she called his name, holding onto him with all her strength as the tremors coursed through them in slowly decreasing spasms of pleasure. She could feel the thundering beat of his heart, and her arms relaxed their fierce grip so her hands could roam down the length of his spine to memorize the sinewed toughness of his back, powerful loins and muscular thighs. "I—I didn't know it could ever be like this," she offered in a trembling, awed voice.

"Only when it's right, my Lindsey. Only when it's between two people who are right for each other." He slid to one side, taking her with him in the cradle of his arms, where he held her tenderly.

"Are we right for each other?" she murmured against the salty, moist column of his corded neck.

"Mmmm, must be. I've never felt like this before either."

Her senses were beginning to return, and Lindsey made an unsteady attempt to pull away from him. But he tightened his hold.

"Oh, Marcus, this is crazy. We've only known each other such a short time."

In an abrupt motion, he released her and stood up. Before she could feel bereft, he scooped her into his arms and headed for his bedroom. "Don't question it. I feel like I've always known you." He set her back on her feet for scant seconds while he drew back the covers, then eased her down between the cool, smooth sheets. He followed her, fitted his body around hers and pulled the coverlet up over them both.

Content and secure in the circle of his arms, she relaxed and drifted into sleep.

7

Lindsey trailed slightly behind Marcus as he carried Kelly into the house, unable to suppress her tears of happiness as the little girl was greeted by her sister and the ladies. Sitting on a big leather chair with her broken leg propped up on the ottoman, Kelly preened under all the attention being given her ungainly white cast. Melodramatically, she explained the plastering procedure as if she had witnessed every second of it. In reality, she had slept straight through the whole thing. Lindsey kept a sharp eye on her, reacting less to the vivid tone of Kelly's voice than to the paleness of her complexion and the dark circles beneath her large brown eyes.

"Kelly can have her cake and lemonade in bed," Elizabeth surprised them all by saying. "That leg needs to rest after all it's been through, and our girl needs some royal treatment for being so brave."

Kelly, who would have normally balked at spending any time during the day in bed, was quick to fall in with Elizabeth's plan. "Yes. I *was* very brave," she agreed. "I hope that my cake is chocolate."

Marcus laughed and lifted her back into his arms, then started for the stairs.

"Is there any other kind?" Althea called after them, reaching down to take Carrie's hand. "Come with me, honey. Let's go make your sister a pretty tray."

"I'm supposed to write my name on her cast." Carrie looked questioningly at her mother. "Shouldn't I do that now?"

"No, Carrie." Lindsey studied her daughter's serious face, sensing that she wasn't quite sure how to handle the situation. She had never needed a stitch, never had a concussion or a broken bone. Carrie always considered carefully before attempting anything that might result in an accident. Therefore, her more reckless sister received a great deal more attention, and today, Kelly was the center of all eyes. "You go with grandma, and then we will all sign Kelly's cast after she's taken a nice nap."

"She's got to take a nap now?" Carrie's blue eyes grew round with astonishment.

"Oh, yes," Lindsey stated emphatically. "Every day until her leg is much better and her head doesn't ache when she's tired."

"Do I have to take a nap too?"

"Not unless you want to," Lindsey said seriously. "You stopped taking naps last year because you don't get grumpy and tired anymore. But Kelly will get very grumpy and tired if she doesn't get lots of rest."

A very unenvious smile lit up the small face. "I don't think I'd like having that old cast on me, not if it means you gotta take naps all the time."

"No, it isn't a nice thing to have at all," Lindsey agreed. "But I know I can count on you to help Kelly through this bad time. I've always been so proud of you for being such a good sister and such a big help to me. I've certainly missed you the last two days."

"You have?" An even brighter smile widened the tiny mouth, then Carrie dropped Althea's hand and ran to her mother for a quick, totally necessary hug and several kisses. "I'd better go help grandma make Kelly's tray. She counts on me too, you know."

"That I do." Althea bestowed a watery smile on them both. "Maggie and Elizabeth are upstairs helping Kelly get settled, Vera's making lemonade, so that leaves me and Carrie to ready the tray."

"Let's use the pretty napkins," Carrie suggested as she took her grandmother's hand.

"What a good idea." Althea cast an approving nod at Lindsey before she was led away into the kitchen.

"Nicely done, Lindsey." Marcus spoke from

behind her. "I didn't think about Carrie's reaction to the homecoming. She's so quiet that everyone forgets she needs attention too."

"Around this house, everyone doles out motherly love." Lindsey shrugged off his compliment and started for the stairs to check on her other daughter. "I don't know what I would've done if they had both wanted me at the same time. Sometimes I can't believe how lucky I am to have my boarders. Did you see how Elizabeth took over? I was so worried about her, but it looks as if she's snapped out of her depression."

"Lindsey." Marcus was following her much too closely and he interrupted her nervous babbling in a no-nonsense tone of voice.

Lindsey reluctantly turned on the bottom step to face him. "What?"

"We need to talk, and now is a good time. The ladies have Kelly well in hand, Carrie is busy in the kitchen, and we won't have much of a chance later on."

"Marcus, I don't think now—"

She wasn't allowed to say more. He grasped her wrist and dragged her into the study. Once inside, he firmly closed the sliding doors behind them and ushered her to the low horsehair couch, taking his place beside her and casually throwing one arm over the back.

Lindsey concentrated on a frayed spot in the carpeting beneath her feet, refusing to give him her full attention. She had gone slightly crazy last night. It was the only explanation for her impetuousness.

She had given Marcus far too much, and she was sure he planned to take even more. She was proven correct with his first words.

"Last night was only the beginning, angel. I hope you realize that."

Still staring at the floor, Lindsey tried to explain the abrupt change in her behavior toward him. As soon as she had awakened this morning, content and drowsily aware of her own sensuality, she had known that she would have to end their relationship. In the bright glare of the morning sun, with his blond head resting comfortably on her shoulder, she had come to terms with her feelings.

She had somehow fallen crazily in love with the man, loved him with a passion she wouldn't have believed possible. To him, she represented hearth and home, family and stability, all the things that were lacking in his life. Being involved with a woman who had children, family commitments, and a handyman's dream of a house was a novelty for him. He was thoroughly enjoying himself in his self-designated role as man of the house. It gave him a great deal of pleasure to charm the ladies, father the children and make love to her, but one day he would decide that he had had enough. When would he require more variety in his life? Another woman? A six-month trip to some faraway place? A new challenge to conquer? Whenever that day came, Lindsey knew she would be devastated, unable to handle it.

Her sobering thoughts had made her behave unnaturally that morning, hiding her fear with a cloak of reserve. Their breakfast conversation had been stilted at best, as she strove to hide her jealousy over "Bunny's" contribution to their meal. He had sprinkled some home-grown parsley over their eggs and told her Bunny thought it made an omelet look more appetizing, thus insuring that Lindsey could not eat a bite. To her, it was only one more proof that there wasn't room for her in Marcus' life. Thinking her silence was caused by the hectic schedule they had to keep, he had blithely gone on making mundane conversation to cover her lapses. When he began to expound on the penchant of Monica, his interior decorator, for dried flowers, and pointed out the various vases placed throughout the room, it merely confirmed her resolution to put distance between them. By the time they were ready to leave for the hospital, Lindsey had made up her mind that, although she loved him, she wouldn't become one of the women in his collection.

"Last night was beautiful for us both." He brought her back to the present.

"Yes, it was, Marcus. But we can't let our physical attraction get out of hand. There is no place for that kind of relationship inside this house. You must see that."

"I can think of lots of places for our kind of relationship." Marcus refused to take her remarks seriously, leaning over and pressing her back against the couch. Before she could push him away, his mouth had commandeered her lips and his hands were playing havoc with her reason. His thumb enticed the wild pulse beating in her throat as his fingers closed tenderly around her slender neck. He kissed his way across one cheek to her ear, sliding her long silky hair away with his hand so he could nibble the soft lobe.

"Mmm." His satisfied voice sent shivers up her spine, and her protests seemed to dissipate like lacy snowflakes melted by a spring sun. "You taste like spiced nectar," he growled huskily, licking and sipping along the sensitive chord of her neck as his hand slipped inside her efficiently unbuttoned shirt-waist to the silk-covered curves of her breasts. It was only when the front clasp of her bra was undone and his mouth had claimed a hardened nipple as his own, that she regained her scattered wits and breathlessly pushed him away.

"Marcus! Stop! What if someone comes in?"

He laughed as if the thought had never occurred to him, ruefully cocking his head to one side as he helped her rebutton her dress. "I doubt we would shock any one of them," he declared with an unabashed grin, brushing her hands away from the front of her dress. "I've made my feelings for you pretty apparent—can't keep my hands off you. Your delectable combination of passion and virtue intoxicates me. That and the way you smell, and taste, and . . ." His hand stroked meaningfully over her bosom. "And feel."

More shocked than she cared to admit, Lindsey slapped his hands away and escaped to the farthest corner of the couch. "I'm sure the older women in this household would attempt to look the other way, but I have two very young and impressionable daughters, Marcus Stafford, and I won't have them walking in on anything like this."

She was sure his loud boisterous laughter could be heard throughout the house and was causing several raised eyebrows. Her cheeks flamed in a fiery red blush and she flashed heatedly, "It's not funny!"

"Yes it is," Marcus disagreed. "Your daughters have already suggested I share your bed, have given me their permission to kiss you and swear that they like me. I wouldn't worry about them, if I were you."

"You know they had no idea what they were talking about when they said those things," Lindsey snapped, outraged that he would use the twins' childish wish to be hospitable against her.

"So, you were eavesdropping on our conversation." Marcus looked smug. "I thought I caught a glimpse of you at your bedroom window when I was getting to know your girls. Of course, I would've rather been kissing their mother coming fresh from a shower. However, I can now corroborate the secondhand information they gave me—their mommy smells good all the time. And all over."

"Of all the—Marcus, don't you dare imply anything like that to anyone else or I'll . . . I'll . . ."

He took pity on her and gave her a playful pat on the knee. "I'm an honorable man, Lindsey. What's going on between us is perfectly natural and doesn't offend anyone. You're the only one who is afraid of what's happening. In the month that I'm here, we'll have to work hard to get you over those fears."

"The month you're here!" Lindsey couldn't believe what she'd just heard. "Nobody said you would be staying for an entire month! I haven't asked you to stay! I think it's a terrible idea. We would end up— No! Absolutely not!"

"You've been outvoted, my prim little lover. I have a month of vacation coming to me, and you have lots of work to be done around here. I have everyone in the house, including your own daughters, on my side."

"We'll see about that!" Lindsey was stung into retorting, the false bravado in her voice apparent to them both. How could she convince the other members of her household that Marcus had to leave? He had probably offered a slew of logical and convincing reasons to continue his stay, and she could tell by the triumphant glimmer in his eyes that she was fighting a losing battle.

"Mommy!" The excited call could be heard approaching from the hall, and Lindsey swiftly jumped off the couch.

"Coming, Carrie," she shouted back, almost running to open the study doors and escape the disturbing presence of her uninvited houseguest. A month! As far as she was concerned it could have been a year. She might be able to withstand Marcus for a minute, a day, but it was going to be impossible to fend him off for a month, and they both knew it.

His amused male laughter followed her up the stairs as she accompanied Althea and Carrie to Kelly's room.

"Isn't that a nice sound to have in the house?" Althea asked the other women as she brought the tray containing a big layer cake and a pitcher of lemonade to Kelly's bedside.

"Uncle Marcus must be happy to live with us," Carrie pronounced matter-of-factly.

"He's not living with us," Lindsey said, far more sharply than she had intended. "He's only visiting."

"My Harry used to laugh like that when he'd ruffled my feathers," Elizabeth recalled fondly, raising a knowing brow in Lindsey's direction. "Don't worry, my dear. He's only joking."

She knew that she should've been elated to hear Elizabeth speaking so calmly about her deceased husband, recalling the good things without tears. But all she could think of was that her last hope of convincing someone to persuade the others against having a houseguest had gone over to the other side.

Vera shouted for Marcus to come upstairs and join them in the celebration. "He loves chocolate cake," she informed them. "Althea, would you make a cherry pie tomorrow? That's another favorite of his."

"Be happy to," Althea agreed, pouring lemonade into Mickey Mouse paper cups. "Maggie, did you bring up the paper plates and napkins?"

"Right here." Maggie helped serve the cake,

handing the plates to the assembled group. The first went to the guest of honor, propped up on her bed.

"You forgot the party hats, ladies." Marcus waltzed into the room and handed out the garish, tri-cornered headgear. "What's a party without hats?"

Everyone fell right in with him, slipping the ridiculous-looking hats onto their heads and adding their voices to his overzealous rendition of "For she's a jolly good fellow."

For some reason, the sight of him prancing about the room in the childish hat, making a total fool out of himself for the pleasure of the pale little girl on the bed, brought a shimmer of tears to Lindsey's eyes. She blinked to keep them at bay, wishing he didn't look so much at home in her house. He was everything she wanted in a man, in a father for her girls, but she knew that to him this was only a passing interlude in his life—one he meant to enjoy to its fullest, then fondly remember when it was over. Could she do that too? Or would she never be able to forget the mischievous bear of a man who enthralled every female in his sphere with his antics?

"Tell Mommy to eat her cake, princess." Marcus wiped a small crumb of chocolate cake from Carrie's mouth with the edge of his thumb. "Otherwise she won't stay as sweet as you."

He sat down on the windowseat and, as if it were the most natural thing in the world, lifted Carrie onto his lap. Two blond heads turned their attention to Lindsey, two pairs of blue eyes staring at her face.

"It's good, Mommy," Carrie decreed. "Grandma made it with her Sunday frosting."

Ignoring the lump in her throat, Lindsey took a healthy bite of the cake and smiled overbrightly at her young daughter. "My favorite kind."

"I think a big ham would do nicely for dinner, Althea." Vera switched the subject to the upcoming meal. "Marcus likes that."

"I thawed out a roast," Althea said, throwing Marcus an apologetic smile.

"No, no," Elizabeth interrupted. "Something nourishing and simple to eat. A nice stew with lots of good vegetables."

"Hot dogs," Carrie chimed in.

"Hamburgers," Kelly declared imperiously. "I get to choose, don't I, Mommy? Don't I?"

"You should have a nice broth," Maggie declared before Lindsey could attempt a mitigation. "Best thing for an ailin' child is broth. Goes down easy."

"I don't want broth!" Kelly cried, her face screwed up in a furious scowl.

"Hold it!" Marcus' resonant male voice brooked no discussion and put a quick end to the rapidly escalating argument. "No one is cooking tonight. Supper's my treat, and I've decided to go out and bring back a big bucket of fried chicken."

Lindsey was completely amazed at the immediate end Marcus had brought to the hostilities.

"Nourishing," Elizabeth approved.

"Best broth's made from chicken," Maggie agreed and patted Kelly's hand. Althea and Vera exchanged smiles of mutual accord while Lindsey shook her head with disbelief.

"Kelly looks ready for her nap," Marcus announced, and again gained everyone's ready agreement.

"Best thing for her," Elizabeth stated in her most professional tone. "Lindsey, you look ready to drop. Why don't you stay with Kelly and try to nap for a few minutes. Take Carrie's bed."

"Good idea." Marcus walked swiftly to the unoccupied bed and pulled down the pink and white checkered spread, asking Carrie's permission to remove the family of stuffed animals who resided there so her mother could lie down. "I know that your mommy hasn't been getting her proper rest," he said wickedly, although it was clear only to Lindsey what he was referring to.

Lindsey didn't like the way he was ordering everyone around, and his teasing was outrageous. "Would everyone stop treating me as if I'm another four-year-old?" she snapped.

"Come on, Carrie," Elizabeth called hastily, rushing the little girl out of the room. "Show me how far along you've come on your puzzle. Mommy's very tired."

Feeling the implied chastisement, Lindsey grimaced as everyone left the room.

"Coming?" Marcus didn't wait for her answer, which would have blistered his ears, but took her hand and pulled her reluctant form to the bed. His eyes challenged her to make a scene in front of the wide-eyed onlooker who watched them from the other bed. Lindsey glared at him, but gave in. He pushed her gently down on the mattress, then solicitously removed her shoes. "I'm getting good at tucking little girls into bed," he teased, knowing she wouldn't retaliate. She held herself stiffly as he pulled the cover up over her and leaned over to plant a loud kiss on her cheek. He then turned away and bestowed the same act of "kindness" on Kelly, telling her that if she were well enough the following weekend, he would take them all on a picnic.

"Can we keep him, Mommy?" Kelly asked in a soft little voice after he left the room. "He's so nice and brings us presents and takes us on picnics and stuff."

"We can't keep people like we do pets." Lindsey sounded relatively calm, but the idea of a caged and domesticated Marcus was highly appealing. She forced a disapproving note into her voice, although she knew she was doing it as a diversionary tactic. "We don't like people just because they bring us nice presents, do we, Kelly?"

She looked across the space separating the two twin beds and found Kelly looking more serious than Lindsey had seen in a long time. One small finger was tucked into the corner of her mouth, and her forehead was creased in a thoughtful furrow. "You know what, Mommy?"

"What?"

"Even if he didn't bring us stuff, I'd like him. " It

was a major concession in his favor, and one Lindsey wasn't sure she wanted to hear.

"Mommy?"

"What?"

"Would *you* like to keep him?"

"Go to sleep, Kelly. We'll talk later. Mommy's tired." She was close to shattering into a million pieces and offered a silent prayer of thanks when Kelly stopped asking questions and closed her eyes.

Oh, I'd love to keep him, all right. Keep him locked up in her room so no other woman could find him. He was overbearing, flamboyantly conceited, but she loved him with all of her heart.

That evening, it was decided that Carrie would sleep in Lindsey's room while Elizabeth spent the night in Kelly's. Lindsey was grateful they had a qualified nurse in the family for she was concerned about the pain Kelly had in her leg. When she was reassured that nothing was out of the ordinary, and after she had settled both of her daughters down for the night, Lindsey walked down the back stairs to the kitchen. So far she had done a good job of avoiding Marcus, and she wanted that to continue.

She knew he had made himself at home in the living room, stretched out on the sofa to watch some ball game on TV and being waited upon like a reclining sheik in an unusually mature harem. He had been given a pillow for his head, a tray for his cold beer and the leftover chicken from supper. A crocheted comforter was placed nearby in case he got cold in the eighty-degree temperature. Unable to watch him without making some cutting

comment, Lindsey walked through the back hallway onto the screened-in side porch. She took a
seat on the old swing, taking comfort in the familiar
creak as she swung back and forth in rhythm with
the music of the crickets populating her garden.
Only the soft glow from the kitchen window illumi-
nated the shadowed porch.

Lindsey relaxed for the first time all day, glad she
had changed into a pair of denim shorts and a
lightweight Daisy Mae blouse. She lifted her legs
onto the seat and curled her bare toes over the
wide arm of the wicker swing as a cooling summer
breeze gathered strength outside.

She closed her eyes, taking a deep breath of the
earthy smell of fresh mint growing in profusion
beside the porch steps, listening to the buzz of
mosquitos through the screens. Although she regu-
larly sought a little peace alone on the porch, she
couldn't enjoy the serenity of her yard as expected.
Instead, the delicate scent of lily of the valley and
the fragrance of oleander reminded her of the
previous night with Marcus. This is my life! she
chided herself. Think of all you'll have to do in the
near future. That will keep your mind off romance!
It would soon be time to gather in the cherries from
the two gnarled old trees behind the house, pick
the big green apples necessary to bake apple pies
for the church picnic, cut down the rhubarb before
it went to seed. She forced herself to think of
familiar things that gave her pleasure, smiling as she
remembered the long, bristled pumpkin vine swiftly

overtaking the small sandbox she had purchased for the twins. The girls had planted the seeds, not realizing that there was a long wait between planting and harvest. They had watched with dismay as the meandering plant had left them no room to play with their toys. She had been unable to convince them to pull up the plant, for they were sure they were growing "The biggest pumpkin in the world."

They all *did* have a good life here. A peaceful life. Her children would grow up healthy and strong. So why wasn't she deriving the usual pleasure at the thought of staying here until they had grown? It was the life-style she had chosen, the one she wanted. She couldn't dream of living anywhere else. She was stupid to even think along those lines, she knew, stupid! stupid! stupid! Had Marcus asked her to join him in the city? Had he asked her to accompany him on the overseas trips he took in his work? No, he hadn't asked her to share his lifestyle, any more than he agreed to share hers. He was momentarily interested in her but would soon move on to other things, other women, other places.

"Everyone else has gone to bed." Marcus stepped out onto the porch and brought her wretched suppositions to a quick halt. "If I went to bed this early, I'd lie there for hours."

Lindsey swiveled on the swing, having little choice but to make room for him as he sat down beside her. "Missing the action in the city?" she asked, trying not to stare at the rippling muscles of his thighs as he used his legs to restart the swaying motion of the swing.

"I was missing you, if you want to know the truth," Marcus neatly sidestepped her slightly petulant question. "You disappeared right after supper and I haven't seen you since."

"It takes time to get two overly tired children ready for bed. I wanted to make sure the twins were asleep before I came back downstairs. Although you looked totally content watching your ball game. I spotted you from the kitchen."

"The Reds lost four to one," Marcus shrugged, insidiously moving his leg closer to hers until they were pushing the swing in unison, her bare skin brushing his denim-clad leg.

"That's too bad." She couldn't have cared less about the baseball score. She needed all of her concentration to maintain a cool front as her heart began pounding with anticipation. She was a pushover, an easy mark! Like a puppeteer with an ingenious knack for pulling the right strings at the right time, he was rapidly overcoming her carefully thought-out reasons for resisting him.

"It's hot out tonight," he said, smiling into her eyes as he began unbuttoning his shirt. He was intent on arousing her and was doing a good job of it as he slowly slipped the buttons from their holes, one by one. Damn the man! It was almost as if he was deliberately taking his time, in order to prolong the pleasure it gave her to watch him.

"Uhuh," she gulped when he pulled the shirt

from the waistband of his jeans and shrugged out of it.

His bronzed arm slid across the back of the swing behind her neck as he moved a fractional space closer. In another minute, her bare arm would come into contact with his tanned chest and then she would be lost. She ran her tongue over her suddenly dry lips. Why? Why didn't she make some excuse and go into the house? Why didn't she tell him to leave her alone?

"Kiss me, Lindsey." The molded sensual mouth was inches away from hers as he closed the space between them and all she felt was the current passing all the way down her side from shoulder to toes. His whispered command only put into words her strongest desires.

Lifting her chin, she stared into the indigo eyes of the man she loved, the man she wanted. Her breath came in tiny pants of excitement as she lifted both hands and framed his face in her palms. "Oh, Marcus, why am I doing this?" she murmured, then took what she needed from him in rapturous response to his husky request. Her pink tongue traced the firm contours of his lips, sought and was given entry, until a passionate truce was declared between their warring tongues and each took their turn pleasing the other.

"It's good to be home, angel." Marcus lifted her across his lap.

But before she could make any comment on his erroneous statement, he was kissing her again, and she was content to let him.

8

〰〰〰〰〰〰〰〰〰

Put me down," Lindsey whispered desperately as Marcus effortlessly carried her through the darkened rooms of the house. But her plea only made him quicken his step. "Marcus, please," she insisted, furtively gazing into the shadows to make sure none of her boarders were walking around the house. Marcus didn't realize how often the women who lived with her would get up during the night because they couldn't sleep. Any minute, one of them could walk down the stairs and interrupt them. Lindsey would die of embarrassment if that happened. Marcus had removed her blouse outside on the porch, and her breasts were pressed against his naked chest. Her hair was a tangled mass, and her mouth was swollen pink by his kisses.

"Thank God no one else sleeps on the first

floor." Marcus nuzzled the soft skin at her nape as he lengthened his stride. "I've been waiting for this all day."

She had to make him listen to her! There was no way she was going to let him make love to her tonight, not here. He lived in the modern-day world where things like this happened all the time, but she, she lived in yesteryear, surrounded by the moral convictions of women who would not understand or condone anyone sleeping together before marriage. Although she was easily as aroused as he, she would not be able to bear the disapproval she would see reflected in the eyes of the women who lived with her if they knew what was going on between her and Marcus.

Marcus carried her into his bedroom, using his shoulder to push the door closed behind him, then striding to the bed. He laid her down on the mattress, giving her barely enough time to bring her palms flat against his chest before covering her with his body and taking her mouth in a breathtaking kiss that left her temporarily stunned. Then she heard the muffled tread of slow-moving feet on the staircase, and she knew she could not let him continue.

Pushing against him with all of her might, she finally made her reluctance to continue clear to him.

"What's wrong?" He rolled off of her and sat up, raking his hand through his hair as he probed her features with a searing blue gaze.

"I—Marcus, this isn't going to work." She

reached for a pillow and held it in front of her, trying not to react to his intense stare. "Not here. I can't make love to you *here*."

"Why the hell not?" He did not attempt to hide his irritation.

"Listen," she begged him, brown eyes dark with regret.

In the long silence that followed, they could both hear the muffled shuffle of slippered feet in the hallway, slowly heading for the kitchen. Thinking no more explanations were necessary, Lindsey tried to get up from the bed, but Marcus grabbed hold of her wrist.

"Where are you going? Nobody knows we're in here. You're a grown woman, and it's nobody's business where you choose to spend the night."

"I didn't choose this, you did," Lindsey pointed out, and was astounded by the immediate stiffening in his body. His jaw clamped rigidly shut, and a polar iciness invaded the blue of his eyes. Never having witnessed Marcus angry before, Lindsey cringed at the barely contained violence she read in his face. He dropped her wrist as if it had been a snake and rolled off the bed. Lindsey swallowed convulsively as he strode to the closet door and jerked it open, then pulled a shirt from a hanger and threw it at her.

"Wear this," he bit out. He turned his back on her as he took another shirt from a hanger and swiftly drew it on. He walked to the door, opened it a crack, then turned to her, glaring at her still naked shoulders. "Hurry up! Whoever is out there is in the kitchen. You should be able to get upstairs without being seen if you go now. I'll go out later and gather up any incriminating evidence we may have left on the porch. Dammit! Get out of here, Lindsey!"

She did exactly that. She was unable to look at him as she edged past him and crept stealthily up the stairs to her room. She felt like a guilty teenager trying to avoid confrontation with a parent.

Once inside her room, she couldn't go to sleep. She was no longer experiencing Marcus' anger, but she'd never forget it. He'd been furious, his tone sarcastic and cold, his eyes contemptuous. Was she being prudish by placing the old-fashioned morality of her boarders ahead of her desire for him? Since she would not go to bed with him in her house, would he pack up and go back to the city where a Bunny or Monica would satisfy his needs? She doubted either of them would have refused what she had refused tonight.

By the next morning she was hollow-eyed from lack of sleep. She was not greatly surprised to hear that Marcus had left Baldridge as soon as he had gotten up that morning.

"He promised to come back on the weekend," Vera informed her as she slid into a chair and accepted a cup of morning coffee. "Said something about having forgotten some calculations he had to make for the man who's overseeing his project while he's on vacation. If you ask me, Marcus can't let go of his work and doesn't trust anyone else to do it for him."

Lindsey struggled to control the cold pain that sliced through her, staring into her cup to avoid the shrewd eyes of her boarders. Althea was busy preparing Kelly's breakfast tray and didn't turn around as she commented, "I thought he planned to replace the pipes in the bathroom today. He wants to be done with that before he takes us on that picnic Saturday."

"He said he'd bring the materials out and start work after the weekend instead," Vera said, taking a chair beside Lindsey at the table. "He did say you'd understand why he had to leave this morning."

Lindsey faltered for an agonized second, then said in an emotionless voice, "Yes. I understand perfectly."

She understood a lot of things now. Her refusal to go to bed with him last night had put a quick end to his obvious plans for her. His final words to her had been the death knell of their relationship. "Get out," he had ordered sharply, but he had been the one to leave, not wasting any more time with a woman who wouldn't give him what he wanted. He had delivered the shopworn promise to return soon, but she knew he wouldn't be coming back. Something would come up to prevent him from coming back for the picnic this weekend—and every other weekend as well. She decided to make it easy for him.

"We shouldn't expect him to use his vacation time working on this house. Please call him, Vera, and tell him that I've already arranged for a plumber to fix those old pipes. He's reasonably priced and I'm sure he'll do a good job. After all, Marcus is a geophysicist, not a plumber."

"Mr. Krebbs on Main Street?" Althea asked, and Lindsey could have kissed her.

"Yes, Grandma." Lindsey put down her cup and stood up from the table. "So you see, Vera, Marcus needn't come back here to waste a perfectly good vacation."

Vera frowned, an odd glint in her eye as she surveyed Lindsey's set features. "Lindsey?" she began hesitantly. "You and Marcus haven't argued, have you?"

"Of course not." Lindsey stubbornly refused to meet Vera's gaze, nonchalantly pushing open the cafe doors. "How could I be angry with a man who's been so much help to us? He's been wonderful with the girls, with me, and I'll always be grateful to him for that." Moving quickly, she released the door and went to the counter, picking up Kelly's tray. "I'll take this up. Make sure you thank Marcus for me when you speak with him. Tell him I hope he enjoys his vacation."

"Yes, dear, I will," Vera returned. But Lindsey doubted she had fooled either of the women. They watched her as she rushed out of the kitchen before she burst into tears.

Later in the day, Vera remarked that Marcus was glad to hear she'd hired someone competent to look at the plumbing and that she'd been correct in her estimation of his ineptitude in that area. No mention was made of his plan to return for the weekend, but she was certain he didn't intend to come. It was just as well, for she knew that she wouldn't be able to endure seeing him again without remembering what it had been like to be held in his arms.

She spent the week enveloped in an unfeeling stupor as she cared for Kelly, placated an envious Carrie and camouflaged her overpowering sense of loss. She had forgotten what it felt like to long for a man's arms around her, listen for an amused male chuckle, wait for a warm gaze to settle appreciatively on her face, but all of those lonely feelings came back in a rush.

Throughout the seemingly endless days, she replayed every minute of time she had shared with Marcus and regretted that she had allowed herself to give in to the desire he inspired in her. All she had gotten for their time together was a deep, painful wound that wouldn't heal and throbbed more painfully every day. With a surge of guilt, she realized that she had never grieved for Peter as she now did for Marcus.

She thought of little else, even knowing it wouldn't have worked, but somehow her heart didn't seem to comprehend what her brain repeated over and over. The interlude with Marcus had been a fleeting thing, a volcanic eruption of desire that consumed her but left nothing but ashes in its wake. What had existed between them had died as soon as he realized she would not give up her outdated scruples to be his lover. That night in his apartment had been not only the beginning, but the end.

By Saturday morning, Kelly was angrily demanding to be allowed out of doors. They had brought her downstairs on the lift Marcus had repaired so she could watch television and play quietly with her dolls. But those activities were no longer enough for her. The entire household was made to suffer for her confinement, and Lindsey was fast losing patience with the whining, belligerent four-year-old who was making miserable everyone who attempted to keep her entertained.

"I hate you, Carrie!" Kelly's high-pitched angry voice was followed by an ominous crash.

Lindsey marched into the room to find out what was causing the commotion and found both of her daughters in tears. Kelly was sniffling from her place on the couch and banging one crutch on the cushions, while Carrie tearfully scrambled across the floor on all fours, trying to pick up the broken china that was scattered across the carpet.

"It's all her fault," Kelly wailed, as soon as she saw her mother. "She won't play with me. She's going to Billy's and I hate her. She's mean and—"

"She threw Georgie at me, Mommy," Carrie defended, sensing that her mother's sympathy might not lie with her sister. "It hit Grandma's vase, the one with the blue flowers on it, and it all broke."

"Carrie, don't touch the pieces. You might cut yourself," Lindsey ordered, bending down on one knee. "Go outside and play until I call you."

Carrie quickly did as she was told, but not before throwing a triumphant glance at her ill-tempered sister. Without looking at Kelly, Lindsey began picking up the slivered pottery from the carpeting. When she had finished, she deposited the fragments in the wastebasket and went to kneel down by the couch. It was time to have a talk with her daughter, the talk she should have had when she realized that Kelly's self-pity was getting worse, not better. She had been so wrapped up in her own troubles she had ignored Kelly's temper tantrums, which had become more and more frequent. Enough was enough.

"It isn't much fun being stuck in the house while your sister goes out to play, is it?"

"I hate her!" Kelly began. But she stopped talking as soon as she saw the ominous expression on her mother's face.

"No, you don't hate her, and I don't want you saying that. Everyone in this house has tried to make things easier for you, especially Carrie. Elizabeth reads you stories, grandma cooks your favorite things to eat, and Carrie hasn't left your side for more than a few minutes until today. I can't say I blame her. Would you like to be with someone who calls you bad names and has forgotten how to say thank you?"

"No," a quavering voice offered an apology. "I'm sorry. I don't like this old cast anymore,

Mommy. I don't like anything." Kelly dissolved into tears.

Lindsey quickly wrapped her arms around her, rocking to and fro until the crying became short, indrawn breaths.

"I know, sweetheart," Lindsey said, "but when we've hurt ourselves, we can't make it better by hurting other people, can we?"

She smiled at Kelly's nod and kept on smiling until she got a smile in return and Kelly hesitantly said, "I have to tell grandma I'm sorry." She was about to start crying again. Lindsey gave her a reassuring pat.

"Grandma will understand, honey. You didn't mean to break her vase." She called Althea and left the two of them together as she walked out onto the front porch. She trusted her not to make things too easy for Kelly, but also to follow any chastise-ment with a full measure of love.

The advice she had given Kelly was some she should have reserved for herself. The situation with her daughter had progressed to this point because she too had been suffering an agonizing attack of self-pity. She felt as much to blame as her daughter for the broken vase. Her responsibilities as a parent had been placed on a back burner while she tried to sort through her own unhappiness. She made up her mind to endure the pain without letting it affect the other members of the household.

But then every logical thought flew out of her head at the sight of a battered jeep pulling into the driveway.

"Oh no," she cried softly. Why had he come back? All of her determination to forget him had been for naught. Every nerve ending in her body came alive as she watched him uncoil his tall body from the seat and begin walking toward the front door. Go away, she wanted to scream. I've just decided to suffer your absence in silence. Don't come back and hurt me again.

Marcus saw her watching him from the porch and tried to restrain himself from breaking into a run. After a week without seeing or talking to her, he felt like taking her into his arms and kissing her senseless. But he knew he would have to be more circumspect. She had made that very clear to him. So he gave himself the treat of surveying her body from head to toe, liking the look of her in close-fitting white shorts and a blue halter.

It was her unwelcoming expression that broke his pleasant train of thought and gave him an unpleasant jolt. Expecting to see the beautiful smile that had haunted him all week, he was surprised by the expressionless mask she wore, which offered him nothing. Suddenly, his hands seemed like two heavy weights on the ends of his arms. He jammed them into the pockets of his jeans.

"Hi, angel." He attempted a smile, cocking his head to one side as he waited for a pleased response.

"The pipes have already been replaced," Lindsey said without preamble. "Didn't Vera phone you?"

She stood carefully to one side as he walked through the screen door, stepping back defensively when he came toward her.

"Is something wrong?"

He advanced another step, and again she retreated. But her voice was amazingly steady when she answered him.

"No. I just didn't expect you. I mean, this isn't the most exciting place to spend a vacation."

"A most loving welcome." His voice was clipped, a shred of anger deepening the rich tone. "You knew I'd be back for the picnic. I promised Kelly." Then he saw Althea's face through the open living room window, and an understanding smile crept over his face. "Don't worry, angel. No heavy clinches until I've done the honorable thing. I promise."

Lindsey was having trouble keeping up with him, his rapid switch in subject was confusing. And today was no different from any other time she had tried to make a point with him. "What do you mean? I have no idea what you're talking about, Marcus Stafford, and I wish you would— Oh!" She gave a tiny cry as he pushed her none too gently ahead of him into the house and gave her an entirely dishonorable slap on the bottom as he walked past her into the living room.

"Ready to go, Rose Red?" he asked the little girl reclining on the couch, who immediately looked as if Prince Charming had just ridden up on his white horse to save the day.

"You remembered." Kelly's brown eyes were nearly as large as Lindsey's as she held out her arms to him and waited for his kiss. He didn't disappoint her, and lifted her up off the couch and into his arms. "Where's Snow White? I need both of my little princesses with me today."

"She's at Billy's. Call her, Mommy," Kelly ordered imperiously, then swiftly remembered the stern lecture she had received earlier and amended, "I mean, would you please call her?"

"I'm not sure," Lindsey began, then gratefully welcomed Althea's timely interruption.

"I packed the picnic basket this morning, so we're all set." Althea's words were followed by the welcoming greetings of the others as they came into the living room. Vera carried a large thermos of lemonade, Maggie held a hamper of food and Elizabeth was clinging to Carrie's hand as she jumped up and down with excitement.

At her first glimpse of Marcus, Carrie skipped across the room and took up position at his side. "Billy wanted to come too, but I told him it was just family."

Marcus accepted that information with aplomb, and didn't even look at Lindsey as he began delivering his plans for the day. He had chosen Deer Creek Park for their picnic and told them to put in the back of the jeep all the essentials for the trip—which to him were food, food and some more food.

As everyone but Lindsey and Kelly scurried to do his bidding, Marcus asked, "You're dressed for a

144

picnic, so why do I get the feeling you weren't expecting me to show up?"

Feeling as if she had been shoved onto center stage without knowing her lines, Lindsey groped for something to say. "I thought," she burst out in frustration, "I thought you'd rather be with Bunny or Monica."

As soon as the names had slipped from her mouth, she could have groaned with dismay. Their impact on him was immediate and humiliating. His loud, booming laugh made Kelly giggle with pleasure, but her mother cringed.

Hearing Kelly's responsive gurgle, Marcus addressed himself to her but his mocking eyes were on Lindsey.

"Your mommy is a funny lady, Rose Red. Now why would I take two happily married ladies to the park when they have their own families to take on picnics? I would much rather take two tiny princesses and their beautiful mother."

Kelly nodded happily in agreement, unaware of the communication taking place on another level between her mother and Marcus. Blue eyes teased and mocked brown ones until dark lashes fell to cover their mortified depths. "Coming, angel?"

Feeling pretty foolish, Lindsey had no choice but to follow them into the hall. She grabbed her purse off the table near the front door and extracted her keys to lock up the house.

Again he was steamrolling her into doing something she had not planned on doing. She was being carried along on a masculine tide as powerful and unrelenting as anything she had ever experienced. All of her doubts were being steadily washed away by the waves of emotion that overcame her whenever he was nearby. Worse, she discovered that she didn't even care.

As she followed him and her giggling daughter to the car, most of her fears were forgotten.

9

~~~~~~~~~~~~~~

In the lush meadow grasses of the clearing, Marcus and Lindsey lay side by side, staring up at the blue sky. As soon as they had finished their picnic lunch and had the twins fully occupied with fishing in the creek, Marcus had led Lindsey away from the family gathering into the surrounding forest. They had discovered the small clearing a few yards off the trodden path.

"See how that cloud is chasing the other?" Marcus pointed. "It's probably a poor male cloud after some fluffy little female."

Lindsey watched as the huge billow overtook a smaller cloud and engulfed it. It was certainly an accurate reflection of her relationship with Marcus. Wasn't he infringing on her space and taking it over? And taking her over? "That little cloud didn't stand a chance," she exclaimed bitterly, closing her eyes to hide the sudden onslaught of emotion that gripped her.

She was vulnerable and defenseless with him. He was bigger, faster and able to do whatever he wanted with her. It was totally unfair! All week she had fought against her feelings for him, and if she wanted to hold on to her pride, she had to gather her strength to go on fighting.

"Hey!" Marcus suddenly noticed that something was wrong, that she was not enjoying their companionable game. "What's the matter, Lindy?"

"Nothing." She swallowed hard and composed her features. "I'm just tired, that's all."

"Are you?"

She looked up to find him leaning over her, his mouth hovering slight inches from hers. While she gallantly tried to fight the losing battle, he took gentle sips of her mouth, awakening the slow-burning embers of passion that never went out where he was concerned. Her small sigh of resignation was lost in a breathless gasp of pleasure as he bared her breasts and muzzled them with his hands.

"This is the feast I had in mind, angel." He released her breasts for the delectation of his mouth, suckling and nipping while she moaned in mounting torment.

"Marcus, Marcus." She couldn't hold back any longer and slipped her hands inside his shirt to feel him, to soothe the overpowering need she had to touch and stroke him as he was doing with her.

They were clasped together in a love-starved embrace when the clear childish voice spoke nearby. "What are you doing to my mommy?"

Both of them froze. Carrie's voice, like an onrush of ice water, broke them apart. Lindsey made a frantic grab for the strings of her halter top as Marcus shifted away from her and sat up to face the curious little girl who sat cross-legged on the ground waiting patiently for an explanation.

While Lindsey fumbled to retie her halter, wondering exactly how much her young daughter had seen, Marcus shielded her from Carrie's inquisitive gaze. Sitting up with his elbows resting on his knees, he addressed Carrie in a somewhat unsteady voice. "I'm trying to convince your mommy that I'd like to be your daddy."

"Would you?" Carrie's serious expression underwent an immediate change to one of pleased wonder. "Would you really like to be my daddy?"

"If your mommy agrees." Marcus glanced over his shoulder at Lindsey, the only sign of his agitation the slight flush that had come up beneath his dark tan.

Lindsey gaped back at him, horrified. This time he had gone too damn far!

"Can he, Mommy?" Carrie scrambled to her feet and threw herself into Lindsey's arms. "He did kiss you on the mouth, so is he going to be our new daddy?"

Too angry and upset to think of anything appropriate to say, Lindsey hugged the child, then firmly set her away from her. "We'll talk about this later, Carrie. Go back to grandma. We'll be there in a little while."

Obediently, Carrie did what she was told. But Lindsey's temper rose well past the boiling point when she heard her daughter's excited voice echoing through the trees: "Grandma! Kelly! Uncle Marcus wants to be our daddy. Mommy's deciding right now."

Lindsey jumped to her feet. "How could you? How dare you!" Her breath came in short, angry pants, her cheeks were dotted with twin spots of fury. Unable to express her complete frustration, she stood clenching and unclenching her hands, glaring at him.

Slowly, Marcus stood up. He didn't meet her eyes as he began rebuttoning his shirt, taking an inordinate amount of time to tuck the loose ends into his jeans. When at last he faced her, his expression was guarded and unreadable. "Getting married is the only practical solution."

"Practical solution? Practical solution!" She was dumbfounded. "To what?" Although she barely came up to his shoulder, her anger was so great she did not even take into consideration the formidable size of her opponent. Using her forefinger to stress each syllable, she poked him repeatedly in the chest. *We are not getting married.*

"Oh yes we are," Marcus contradicted.

His calm, confident statement was the last straw. With all the force she could muster, she leaned back in a rage and took aim with her fist. As her arm came forward to knock the breath from his body, he caught her wrist to avoid the blow. Efficiently, he grasped her elbow and pulled her against him.

"Your halo is slipping, sweetheart. What angel would punch a mere mortal man in the stomach?"

"You are not talking your way out of things this time, Marcus."

"Talking isn't how we got into this," he stated firmly, staring down at her outraged face. He refused to let her go. She struggled uselessly, trying to kick at him, until he tightened his hold even more and she had to stand still in order to breathe.

"To uphold your old-fashioned honor, I'm prepared to do the right thing. You've been compromised, and believe me, next time could be worse. If you don't want your family to walk in on us again, let's marry up all legal and proper."

"That's ridiculous," she raged. "This is the twentieth century."

"That's a convenient excuse." He gazed skywards as if he might find answers in the clouds. "One day you're too straitlaced to consider sleeping with me, the next you're too modern to get married. You can't have it both ways, Lindy. How do you want it, with or without a ring?"

Appalled, Lindsey resorted to begging. "You can't do this to me, Marcus. Please, let me go." Crushed against him, her body couldn't deny what her brain proclaimed loud and clear.

"Feel what you're capable of doing to me," Marcus flared gruffly. Grasping her hips, he pulled her to him leaving her in no doubt of his needs.

Brown eyes, wide with shock, winced in the shadow of his descending head and fluttered closed when his marauding mouth took ruthless command of her parted lips. He took a guided tour of her, using his tongue, lips and hands to locate and explore every sensitive area. When she fiercely refused to give in to her feelings, he led her astray by taking her hands and moving them over the evidence of his mounting desire. A hot rush of wanting marked her defeat as he brought one hand behind her and lifted her against him. She vibrated with heated response, molding herself between the taut muscles of his thighs.

She was shattered when he jerked away from her, taking in huge gulps of air.

"I could drag you off to the bushes and you wouldn't have said a word," he pointed out brutally. "Now do you see we've got no other choice?"

Her answer was barely audible. "We hardly even know each other. What will people think?"

"The people who count won't think anything." He stepped toward her and took her hand. "Come on. Carrie's probably got us past the altar by now."

Lindsey stumbled along behind him for several yards, too distraught to feel the sharp branches that caught on her clothes and scratched her legs. When she had regained some control over herself, she pulled away from him. "No, Marcus! This isn't right, not for me."

He was in no mood for further arguments, but she held her ground as he fixed her with a paralyzing ice-blue gaze. "It had better be right! You'll have a father for your children, a live-in handyman and a lover who satisfies you. What more do you want?"

Your love! her mind shouted, crying the words she couldn't say out loud. The dejected slump of her shoulders was proof of her inability to fight him any longer. He had won; she had lost.

Marcus took one look at her tormented brown eyes and the heart-rending droop of her figure and couldn't move. Half angry, half ashamed, he clenched his fists, then stepped toward her and grasped her by the arms, staring deep into her pain-filled eyes.

"I want you, Lindy, and I know you want me. I'll give you time to reconcile yourself to it, I promise, but we do have to put up some kind of front for the family. Can you imagine what they'll think if you and I don't say something about what Carrie has told them? Ours is an unorthodox situation, which I'm doing my best to make proper and acceptable to both you and them. Help me, Lindsey, because I don't think I can stand it much longer."

The raw pain in his voice was her undoing. "Everything's happening too fast," she whispered, leaning her cheek against his chest. She comforted herself by listening to the strong beat of his heart, the feel of his hands gentle on the back of her head. "I do want you Marcus, but . . . this isn't right."

Looking up, she tried to express her feelings, her doubts. "We've barely met, and there are so many problems we haven't even talked about."

"I know everything I need to know." Marcus

lifted her chin and placed a soft kiss on her lips. "My mother is a voracious writer and I have letters and letters on one Lindsey Delaney. This week I discovered that I need her quite badly and want her desperately. So much that I'd do almost anything to get her."

"But marriage—"

"I want a home and a family," Marcus interrupted. "I used to dream about coming back from my trips to a wife and a house full of laughing children instead of to my lonely apartment. Give me that dream, Lindsey, please."

"I'll have to think about it, Marcus," she said, trying to hide her hurt.

She had known all along that the major attraction he felt was her life-style. Could she marry a man when she knew that he didn't love her but rather wanted her and all she represented to him? Wanted to play the role of father to her children? Wanted the security of a family waiting for him to come home? Hadn't that been what she had had with Peter and promised herself she wouldn't accept again?

Her thoughts were in turmoil but she did admit that Marcus was a much more affectionate man than her late husband. Perhaps she should marry him to benefit the children who wanted a daddy so badly.

"In the meantime, you'll go along with our ill-timed engagement?"

"Up to a point." She gave in, deciding to give

him that much until she had more time to think about it.

The instant they arrived back at the picnic area, she regretted that decision. The expectant looks on the women's and children's faces made her feel guilty and uncomfortable. But Marcus didn't appear to have similar qualms. He squeezed her shoulder, smiled affectionately at everyone and drew Lindsey forward. "We haven't set a date yet, so don't start baking a wedding cake."

"Marcus!" Lindsey exclaimed, not expecting him to make it sound as if a good time for the wedding was all that was keeping them apart. Hadn't he listened to a single word she had said?

"But Uncle Marcus is going to be our new daddy, isn't he?" Two beaming faces raised worried eyes to their mother.

The answer the children wanted was also anxiously awaited by the four women seated around the picnic table, no longer bothering to hide their interest. Lindsey's glance darted from one face to the next. Although Vera and Althea had led the group in their matchmaking efforts, she noticed that they appeared to be the only ones who showed any misgivings. Maggie and Elizabeth were smiling like two Cheshire cats, but Vera and Althea exchanged apprehensive glances as Lindsey groped for some vague response that would satisfy her daughters.

However, it was not Lindsey but Marcus who answered them. Bending down on one knee before the twins, he said quietly, "Your mommy and I still have a lot of talking to do. Grown-ups need time to decide important things, and becoming your daddy is very important to me. Your mother and I must think very hard and make sure everything is right. So, until we have talked over everything, I'll go on being your Uncle Marcus. O.K.?"

His serious tone impressed the twins, and the two girls solemnly nodded their heads in unison.

"Good," Marcus approved. "Then let's go see if we can catch us some fish. Have you had any bites?"

"Maggie cut up our worms real small 'cuz she said we were wasting them. The fishies don't like small food like that, Uncle Marcus." Kelly lifted her bamboo pole so he could see the bare hook. "They spit it right out."

Lindsey released her pent-up breath, pleased that her children were so easily distracted. Under other circumstances she would have smiled as Marcus exchanged an understanding grin with Maggie over the tops of the twins heads.

"Let's go see if they'll bite on a great big worm then, shall we?" he suggested.

"Me too?" Carrie asked, tugging on his large hand.

"You too. And your mother." Marcus didn't show it, but Lindsey gained the decided impression that he didn't want her discussing her true feelings with her boarders outside his hearing. "Coming, Lindsey?"

Since she didn't want to talk about it any more than he did, she quickly agreed. She gathered up

Carrie's pole and the container of worms as Marcus lifted Kelly and began walking toward the large boulders that were strewn along the banks of the slow-moving creek.

"I want to talk with you, Marcus," Vera shouted after them. But Marcus didn't falter a step in his stride or look back once.

"We'll talk later, Mom," he called over his shoulder. "We've got some serious fishing to do here."

"Hmmph." Lindsey heard Vera's annoyed exclamation but she didn't dare look back either, sure she would see the same kind of frustration on the face of her grandmother. With as much dignity as possible, she ignored the immediate buzz of conversation that erupted behind them.

Marcus gave her a self-derisive grin as he placed Kelly down on a flat-edged rock and adjusted her cast in a comfortable position. "Always put off until tomorrow what you're too cowardly to face today."

"They're just concerned." Lindsey darted a quick glance back at the picnic table and groaned under her breath at the sight of four heads bent closely together. "I can imagine what they're saying."

"I hope they're not plotting a shotgun wedding. From the looks of you, you've been well and truly—" He broke off with his teasing when he saw that two little girls were hanging on his every word. He cleared his throat. "Get your lines in the water, ladies. How else do you expect to catch any fish?"

"We need some worms, Uncle Marcus," Carrie reminded, shaking her head. She appeared to have doubts that he was going to turn out to be any more a proficient fishing instructor than Maggie.

Sheepishly, Marcus reached for the container of worms, rolling his eyes expressively at Lindsey. "I'm beginning to think I've lost every bit of intelligence I once had. I used to be a thorough, detailed and methodical person, but look what's happened to me."

Lindsey was too busy pulling the leaves from her hair and brushing off her clothes to show any sympathy for him. "I'm far more concerned over what's happened to me," she declared, frowning at the image she must have presented to the four women now discussing her at the picnic table.

"Hurry up, Uncle Marcus," Kelly complained from her perch on the rock.

"Yes, hurry." Carrie's tone echoed that of her sister's.

Lindsey glanced up and caught an odd expression on Marcus' face before he swiftly turned away and began to bait her daughter's hooks. What had that look conveyed? Was it concern? Regret? Was he finally comprehending how complicated things had become and how difficult it would be to extricate themselves from the impossible predicament he had inadvertently precipitated? Or had it been deliberate? Did he want to force her into marrying him? No, he wasn't that kind of man. If he had stopped for one minute and considered the consequences, he would never have told Carrie that he was hoping to become her daddy to justify kissing Lindsey in the eyes of her daughter. Unfortunately, the little girl had taken him at his word, and now they would all have to pay for it.

"Look, Mommy, look!" Carrie jumped up and down on the shore, swinging her fishing pole over the placid blue-gray water. "I caught one, I did. I really did."

"Trophy size," Marcus proclaimed, grabbing Carrie's line and measuring the wiggling bluegill that dangled from it with his hands. "Want to cook him for supper, honey?"

"Oh, no." Carrie looked horrified. "We can't hurt him." Her blue eyes filled up with tears as Marcus' brows rose.

"What do you want to do with him, then?" he asked, totally bewildered by the child's emotional entreaty.

"Let him go, Uncle Marcus," Kelly demanded succinctly. "He never did anything to you."

"Yes, Uncle Marcus." Lindsey placed her hands on her hips and smirked. "He didn't do anything to you. How could you want to eat that sweet little fish?"

"Sweet little . . ." Marcus spluttered for an answer, glancing from one pair of accusing feminine eyes to the next. "Women!" he finally pronounced disgustedly. "You'd all starve to death if men felt that way."

"No we wouldn't," Carrie disagreed.

"And why not?"

"'Cuz Mommy buys our food at the store all the time."

Taken aback by her four-year-old logic, Marcus

threw up his hands. "So she does." With an amazingly gentle touch, he unhooked the fish from Carrie's line and threw it back into the creek. "Now what?" he asked them when the silvery fin had disappeared beneath the surface of the water to swim away out of sight.

"I don't want to fish anymore," Kelly adamantly declared. "It's mean."

"All right." Marcus helped them reel in their lines and removed the bait from their hooks. Lindsey tried to keep a straight face at his disgruntled expression as he efficiently wrapped the lines around the poles and handed them to her, muttering under his breath. Without saying another word to the children, he picked up Kelly and began walking back to the picnic area.

"Are you pouting, Uncle Marcus?" Kelly asked, as she tightened her hold around his neck.

"Men don't pout," he retorted, clearing his throat gruffly. "Sometimes we get a little confused, but we don't pout."

"Billy pouts." Carrie trotted after him, her short legs having difficulty keeping up with his long stride. "But I guess he's not a man yet."

Lindsey followed the threesome at a distance. Again, as she had the day of Kelly's homecoming, she was struck by the picture he made with her daughters. The sight of Kelly's small brown hands clasped tightly around his neck and Carrie trying to match his male step formed a huge knot in the region of her heart. Her daughters loved him, and so did she. She wondered how many times she would have to admit that to herself before she allowed herself to accept it and, once accepting it, take what he was offering to her.

When they reached the picnic area, Marcus placed Kelly on the blanket that had been spread out on the ground. He drew Carrie down beside him and took up a cross-legged position. "It's almost time to pack up and go home. Did you like our picnic?"

"It was fun, 'ceptin' the fishing part," Carrie acknowledged with a shy smile. "Are we going to come here again sometime?"

"I hope so." He glanced up at Lindsey, then away. "I want to ask you two something."

"What?" the two children demanded at the same time.

"I'd like to take your mommy out on a date tonight. Would you girls mind if I steal her away from you for a little while? Can she come with me to Columbus tonight?" He cocked his head at the four women blatantly eavesdropping on his conversation with the twins. "Would you watch these two for us if I take Lindsey out for the evening?"

"Of course," Althea said at once. "I think it would be a good idea for the two of you to have some time alone. Apparently, you have a great deal to talk about."

Marcus winced slightly at Althea's concerned expression, and Lindsey was amazed when he stood up from the blanket and walked over to the woman, extending his hand to help her up from the picnic table. He drew her away from the others, but

Lindsey couldn't overhear him as he began speaking to her grandmother.

Everyone else began gathering up the remnants from the picnic, policing the area to make sure they left the grounds in the same condition in which they had found it.

While they all worked to get ready to leave, Lindsey began thinking about her grandmother, concerned over the possibility of her wrongly deciding that she and the other women might be standing in the way of Lindsey's future happiness. She recalled how it had been with Peter, how he had made it clear that Althea wasn't welcome in their home. Were her boarders wondering if they would be asked to leave once Lindsey remarried?

She didn't realize she was holding up the others, or that Marcus was standing silently beside her, watching her, until Althea picked up the picnic basket and told the others to start for the car. "Elizabeth and Maggie can get Kelly settled in the back seat. You two come when you're ready."

"Thank you, Mrs. Patterson." Marcus gripped Lindsey's arm above the elbow, his smile never slipping as he gritted to her between his teeth, "Will you stop looking like there's just been a death in the family."

As soon as the others had passed out of hearing distance, Lindsey said, "I won't have them hurt, Marcus. If I do marry again, every one of them will be a part of my household. Let's make that clear from the beginning."

"Let's go to the car," Marcus ordered grimly. "We will discuss all of this later, but now is not the time." He hesitated, a strange expression passing over his face, then he informed her gruffly, "I didn't plan on this happening. I swear it."

Lindsey turned away so he wouldn't see how much his harsh statement had hurt her. Of course she knew that. She was fully aware that he hadn't planned what had happened, painfully conscious of the fact that he wasn't the kind of man who would ask a woman to marry him just to gain a bed-partner. No, he planned to acquire much more from her than that.

Since he had inadvertently precipitated a situation that required a proposal, he had made one, and then had evidently decided to make the best of it. He had reached the stage in his life when he wanted a home and a family. Because he had foolishly blurted his wishes to her daughter, Lindsey knew there was every likelihood he would get his wish. He was an honorable man and would do the honorable thing. Perhaps, if they hadn't made love, Lindsey would have insisted he extricate them from this situation, but she had little pride anymore where he was concerned. She went willingly into his arms at the slightest urging, desperately hoping that his desire for her would one day turn into the same kind of love she felt for him. In the little time she had known him, he had thrown her whole life into turmoil. It was desolate contemplating a return to the placid existence she had enjoyed before he had come. Even hearing him admit that he hadn't planned on marrying her, she couldn't bear the thought of losing him.

Didn't you learn anything the first time around, Lindsey? Don't you remember how quickly passion turns into complacency? How swiftly Peter's desire died into perfunctory obligation? Could she go through that again?

"We're leaving, Lindsey." Marcus took her by the arm and escorted her to the car, his face cast into a granite mask. She stared sightlessly out the car window the entire way back to Baldridge, not seeing the frequent glances at her averted profile being delivered by the driver.

It took her little more than an hour to prepare herself for the evening ahead. When they entered the house, Marcus told her to wear something casual, and she took him at his word. Putting on a straight linen skirt that buttoned up the side and a flowered print silk blouse, she glanced in the mirror on her closet door and decided she looked remarkably calm for a woman who was contemplating getting married to a man who did not love her. Her brown eyes showed none of the anxiety she was feeling, her skin was glowing from an afternoon spent in the sun and her face showed none of the mental anguish she was experiencing. Perhaps her body had gone into some kind of shock, refusing to reflect her inner turmoil. Occasionally she could hear Marcus' deep laugh interspersed with that of her children; the sound never failed to make her feel happy. She was a fool, but she was beginning to think she would have to resign herself to that condition.

She was brushing her hair when a knock came on the bedroom door and Althea came in. She sat down on the bed, watching Lindsey closely before she said what she had come to say.

"Do you feel as happy as a young woman should who has just received a marriage proposal?"

Lindsey replaced the hairbrush on her vanity, and swiveled around on the small stool. "Nothing that definite, Grandma. This whole thing started because Carrie saw Marcus and me kissing. I don't know why he told her . . ."

"What exactly did he tell her?" Althea asked.

"He said he was trying to convince me to let him be her daddy." Lindsey began unconsciously twisting her hands in her lap. "I'm sure he regrets every word of it now."

Althea emitted an amused chuckle. "I sincerely doubt that, Lindsey. Anyone with eyes in their heads could take one look at him and tell he'd lost his heart."

"Grandma!" Lindsey cried, shocked. "I've only known him a week! I went with Peter for two years before we even thought about getting married. Marcus can't possibly love me."

"Why not? You love him, don't you?"

"Yes, but . . ."

"No buts," Althea stated firmly. "What you felt for Peter and feel for Marcus are two entirely different things, aren't they?" She accepted Lindsey's small disbelieving nod as her answer and went on. "Don't throw away this chance for happiness because you think it's happened too quickly. We don't choose who we love or when it will happen. You know Marcus very well, if you think about it. I think Vera has good reason to feel proud of him. He's a fine man."

"You approve?" Lindsey couldn't have been more surprised, and her startled look made Althea laugh.

"You certainly are too old to require my approval, but you have it. I think Marcus is a perfect match for you."

"But . . . I thought . . ."

"You thought I was worried about the possibility of losing my home. Marcus would no more ask any of us to leave here than you would. He isn't Peter, honey, so stop comparing the two of them. Follow your heart," Althea advised wisely. "The only thing that concerns me is you throwing away what you want and need because you think it's too soon or that it might offend your family. I find Marcus' inability to hide his feelings for you quite refreshing."

It took Lindsey a full half an hour to get over what her grandmother had stopped by to tell her. She replayed every word in her head. Was her grandmother right? Had she been comparing Marcus with Peter and letting the failures of her first marriage jeopardize her chances in a second? Althea made it sound as if Marcus might truly care for her, possibly even love her, but Lindsey couldn't believe it. Home, family, children and a willing woman to hold in his arms were the things he desired; love didn't come into it.

One minute she could talk herself into believing he had fallen in love with her as quickly as she had fallen for him, and the next she had talked herself out of it.

Finally, she decided to carefully consider every step she took in advance and not make any decisions until she was certain of Marcus' feelings.

A short while later, she finished saying her good-nights to the twins and went downstairs to find Althea and tell her she was ready to leave. As she descended the back steps to the kitchen, she heard voices, and when she got closer, recognized them as Vera's and Marcus'. Vera had finally found the opportunity to corner her son, something Marcus had managed to avoid all afternoon but obviously had not been able to avoid all together.

Lindsey smiled to herself, intending to retreat back up the stairs and give them some privacy. Then she heard him angrily speak her name. She could not hear the muffled phrase that followed but was compelled to walk down another step so she could pick up what they were saying.

"What a mess you've made of it," Vera reproved angrily, slamming a cupboard door.

"Mother!" Marcus interjected in an exasperated tone. "It's far too late to do anything about it now. I'll work on the love part after we're married."

Lindsey heard the sincere regret in his voice and wanted to curl up in a tight ball of misery. He didn't love her but hoped that would come later on.

167

"You'll answer to me if you hurt that young woman," Vera admonished sharply. Lindsey could not recall ever hearing her sound more irate. "I never thought I'd say this, Marcus, but I'm disappointed in you."

"No more disappointed than I am in myself," Marcus spoke so softly that Lindsey had to strain to hear him. "Lindsey is a fine woman, and all I can do is promise to make things right."

"See that you do," Vera commanded. "And as quickly as possible."

Neither person in the kitchen heard Lindsey utter a small gasp of pain and stagger back up the stairs. When she joined Marcus in the car fifteen minutes later, her mind was beginning to function again but she felt empty, empty and miserable. After the conversation she had overheard, there was no doubt left in her mind. She would break things off with Marcus before they got any further out of hand. He had practically been ordered to protect the reputation of the "fine woman" he had supposedly besmirched, but she would convince him there was no reason to go through with it. Eventually, he would have resented having "had" to marry her, resented both her and his mother, and she couldn't let that happen.

During the thirty-minute drive to Columbus, they sat quietly, increasingly aware of a mounting strain growing between them. Surreptitiously, Lindsey glanced at his silent profile. There was not a hint of a smile on his brooding features, not a trace of amusement in his compelling blue eyes. Unaware of her inspection, he was concentrating on the highway, a muscle occasionally clenching along his strong jaw.

Unable to stand the nerve-racking silence, Lindsey finally ventured a soft question. "Where are we going?"

Without taking his eyes from the road, Marcus snapped, "I'm taking you to my place, where we can talk without interruption. I don't want to cause any more *accidents* today, so let it alone until we get there, would you?"

Feeling as if he had slapped her, Lindsey's eyes filled with tears. She turned abruptly away to stare out the car window. She didn't offer another word as they completed the drive to his apartment.

10

~e~e~e~e~e~e~e~e~e~

Leaning back against the large velvet cushions of the conversation pit, Lindsey gazed up through the wide skylight to the stars. If she had any faith in superstition, she would have liked to make a wish on one of the shining silver pinpoints of light. But dreams did not come true for wishing. Instead, she switched on a nearby lamp to dispell the romantic atmosphere and rid herself of the passionate images she had of herself and Marcus making love in the moonlight. She was glad that she had been given a few minutes to gather her mental energy while Marcus took a shower and changed clothes.

Nervously anxious, she had barely managed a weak smile when he had ushered her into the apartment and pointed out the various remains of their picnic spotting his clothes. It was difficult for her to look at him at all, knowing that tonight would be their last night together. She would set him free. She could not marry a man whose only reason for marrying her was because he felt honor bound to save her reputation with a group of older women. She had to convince him to forget his rash pseudo-proposal and think of some way to appease his old-fashioned mother who expected him to go through with it.

Deep in thought, she drew her legs up underneath her skirt and tilted her head back, looking as if she might find solutions to her problems written across the dark sky.

When Marcus walked into the room a few minutes later, Lindsey had not moved from her position. His eyes darkened when he saw her, curled up on the cushions, hugging herself as if she were cold. Her large brown eyes were troubled and wary, her expression uncertain. She seemed to him like a cautious kitten, longing to be stroked yet fiercely independent. A beautiful creature who had far too much pride to let anyone force a decision upon her that she had not yet made for herself.

He knew he had made a grave mistake that afternoon as soon as the words had been said, but Carrie's timely interruption had seemed such a golden opportunity for him to achieve what he wanted without delay. Unfortunately, he had momentarily forgotten that Lindsey wasn't the type of woman to react favorably to such high-handed methods. He knew he was facing an uphill struggle that might end with her walking out on him for good.

He gave himself the luxury of watching her for a few more moments, then went to join her. "Are you going to forgive me, Lindsey?"

Lindsey jumped like the startled cat he had likened her to, and tried not to flinch away when he came down beside her, stretching out his long legs before him. He propped himself up on both elbows and stared at his shoes, not looking at her as he waited for her answer.

Intensely aware of his proximity, she wasn't sure how to respond. Unwillingly, her eyes traveled down the length of him from the cream-colored knit sport shirt tucked into his pants at his slim waist, over the narrow hips and then down the taut brown material covering the powerful muscles of his legs. "Marcus . . . I don't . . ."

"You don't want to be stampeded into marriage." He completed the sentence for her. "You want us to follow the traditional road. Love, then marriage and after a year or so a baby carriage. Well, it didn't work out that way for us, Lindsey, and I can't see any way of changing that."

"That wasn't what I was going to say, but since you've brought it up, I don't want to settle for any less than that, no." She sat up straight and clasped her arms over her breasts, pressing her body upright against the pillows. She expected him to sit up too, but he maintained his nearly prone position, continuing his intense contemplation of his expensive leather shoes. It was going to be very difficult to conduct the conversation Lindsey had planned in the informal setting of the pit, especially if he insisted on lying down.

"How much time do you want?" he asked quietly, a nonchalant question that had such a bitter edge to it that Lindsey quailed.

"It isn't a question of time." She bit her lip, then shut her eyes and said what needed to be said. "I've no intention of marrying you, now or later."

After a long, drawn-out silence, Marcus said in an uncharacteristically low voice, "I see."

His tone reminded Lindsey of the dangerous cutting edge of a sword as he went on.

"You're going to throw it all away, aren't you? Just because I couldn't toe the line, couldn't keep my feelings under control like you expect any respectable man my age should be able to do."

He did sit up then, but Lindsey suddenly wished he hadn't. The impact of his blue eyes boring into her was devastating. She paled to the color of chalk as he placed both of his hands on her shoulders, his grip like iron biting into her. "What about you, Lindsey? Can you deny that you want me so badly it hurts?"

He forced her back upon the cushions and followed her down, stretching himself full length upon her. With his indigo eyes fastened hungrily on her parted lips, she could not find words to deny him, could not withstand the feel of his demanding hardness pressing against her.

"Marcus," she whimpered, trying to breathe but

robbed of everything but the need to hold him, to feel the taut lines of his body as she had done once before in this exact spot. Her arms came up to reclaim possession of him, clinging to his neck as she drew his mouth down to hers. Within seconds she was aflame, her desire for him igniting as quickly as always. Without thinking about what her fervent answer implied, she responded to his urgent questing tongue.

Her well-thought-out speech was forgotten in their delirious exchange of drugged kisses. With him she was no longer a conformist clinging to tradition but an innovator, an uninhibited feminine creature who needed to show him all she knew of giving and loving.

"Is there anything wrong with this kind of feeling?" he demanded huskily, rolling to one side in order to slide her silk blouse away from her shoulders. His warm mouth paid homage to her breasts, his hands stroked the quivering curves.

Lindsey softly murmured, "No, Marcus, no," so he wouldn't stop the exquisite pleasure it gave her. She was as eager as he to remove the constricting garments that had become unacceptable barriers between them and in seconds, the vibrating agony of anticipation became a breathy sigh of fulfillment as his aroused male force pressed against her waiting femininity. His knee wedged between her thighs, making her ache with yearning, but he was intent on inciting every nerve to the same fever pitch.

She was equally as thorough, seeking and finding all the satiny steel and hard smoothness of his male perfection, reveling in the shudders of response her touch inspired in him. "You can make me want anything," she groaned.

Her words brought a swift and unbelievable end to the soul-shattering pleasure she was certain had been only seconds away. His spine went rigid, and he pushed himself off her, reaching for his trousers and standing up to pull them on.

"Dammit, Lindsey, not this time," he savagely snarled at her, going down on his knees to face her. Holding her shocked eyes with his, he grabbed his shirt and pulled it around her. His breath sounded as ragged as hers, but he guided her arms into the sleeves and securely buttoned up the front. "I promised myself I wouldn't use sex to ramrod you into making a decision, but I could—and we both damn well know it."

His sarcastic words were so patently true that Lindsey could think of nothing but escape. "I'm getting out of . . ." She searched frantically around her for her own clothes but he appalled her even more by angrily snatching them away out of her reach.

"You're staying until we get this thing settled!" he snarled. Minutes before he had been an impassioned lover, but the passion had gone and now he was all aggressor, issuing harsh commands and daring her to defy him.

In all the time she had known him—which she

knew wasn't that long—she had never once felt truly afraid, but she did now, and it showed on her face. She backed away from him, looking like a cornered animal as she stared back at him with terrified eyes.

The look on her face seemed to cause him some sort of pain, for his shoulders slumped and he sank back on his heels, clasping his hands together between his knees. "Don't you know what you're doing to me?" he asked in a tortured voice that completely bewildered her. Why did it sound as if she were the one hurting him when he had been the one to reject her? When he lowered himself to the carpeting, taking deep breaths and holding his head in his hands, she didn't move, warily waiting to see what he would do next.

She was accustomed to a teasing, charming or passionate Marcus, but this angry, defeated even vulnerable-looking man was outside her experience, and she didn't quite know what to do. Because she loved him, she had an irresistible urge to comfort him. Swallowing her pride, she crawled across the space separating them and tentatively placed her hand on his shoulder.

Violently, he twisted away from her and ordered roughly, "Don't touch me, Lindsey! My body longs to tell you everything there is to say, but dammit, you have to have the words or it won't solve anything."

"I don't understand you, Marcus." She didn't move away from him, caught by the urgency and pain in his voice. "What words?"

He countered her question with one of his own. "Why do you think I want to marry you, Lindsey?"

What did he want her to say? Did he require verbal confirmation of her desire for him? Did he think she needed to be told how much he wanted her when he had just shown her? She knew he desired her, had known from the beginning, but she wanted more from him. He wasn't aware that she wanted his love. "I'm sure you want to do right by me, Marcus."

His dismissing laugh jarred her as much as the contemptuous look on his face. She didn't understand his anger, didn't comprehend why he took her acknowledgment of his high moral caliber as an insult.

"Get dressed, Lindsey. Then you and I are going into the kitchen and sit down on opposite sides of the table. I'll present my case, and when I've finished, you can present yours."

"This isn't something we can negotiate." Her bewildered expression did not bring a smile, but he did elaborate.

"I think it is, but since it's apparent I can't keep my hands off you long enough to say a logical word, we're going to have an obstacle between us until the talking is done. You are the most obtuse woman, Lindsey! As far as I'm concerned, this whole damn exercise is unnecessary."

"Well, that's fine by me," Lindsey retorted, hurt by his unexpected assault. "Calling me names is no way to foster a conversation, so I think we'll call off this 'whole damn exercise,' if you don't mind."

"You'll get dressed and listen to me or I'll prove my point by making love to you until you've absolutely nothing left to say. I've tried to be patient, Lindsey, but no more. We are here for the duration, whether you like it or not."

Lindsey was about to utter another dismissive sally, but the savage look on his face and the threatening step he took toward her dried the words in her throat. While she swiftly went to do what he asked, he stalked into the kitchen and placed a pot of coffee on the stove. She delayed continuing their bewildering dialogue by holing up in the bathroom. He must have guessed that was her intention, for his booming voice resounded through the door.

"You've got until the coffee is done to present yourself in the kitchen."

She suspected he wouldn't think twice about breaking the door down to enforce his words, so she hurriedly used the short time allotted to comb her hair, straighten her clothes and splash cold water on her face.

Gazing into the mirror, she viewed her hunted brown eyes and passion-bruised lips with dejection. What did Marcus want from her? She could hear him slamming around in the kitchen and was profoundly aware he was still in a rage. What had caused his physical rejection of her and the impassioned speech that followed? He wasn't making much sense. When she heard the ominous sound of coffee mugs being placed on the table, none too gently, she knew her time was up. Perhaps without her realizing it, he had reached the same conclusions as she had, and the forthcoming conversation was to mark the end of their involvement. Maybe he thought that by making her angry, she wouldn't be hurt when he told her he had only wanted an affair not a lifelong commitment.

"Get out here, Lindsey," Marcus called.

Taking a deep breath, she went to face the inevitable.

They had never behaved quite as awkwardly with one another before, and they both moved stiffly as they took their seats at the table. At first, they each sat silently, sipping their hot coffee to avoid making eye contact. Then Marcus began speaking in a gentle tone, devoid of all anger, a tone that got Lindsey's full attention.

"You're everything I want in a woman, Lindsey. The timing is rotten, and I know that bothers you, but we're both mature adults who shouldn't have to play these games anymore. I want to marry you, be a father to your twins and help you care for the women who share your home. I think you want me too, but are afraid to take what I'm offering. I wish I had more time for conventions, but when I'm with you I'm not capable of rational behavior. I want us to get on with it, Lindsey. Right now, before I go completely out of my mind."

"Don't you hear how that sounds?" Lindsey couldn't hold back any longer. "I'll admit we have something between us—a kind of passion for one another that's different from anything I've ever felt before. But it erupted much too fast, and I'm sure it'll die the same way."

He opened his mouth to contradict her, but she held up her hand. "I've watched you win over my girls, charm my boarders, and survey the house as if you can't wait to start repairing all that's wrong with it. You've won me over too, but I'm smart enough to know that it isn't me you really want. You're in love with the idea of a permanent home, a family and a wife. I don't blame you for wanting all of those things, but I've already been through that kind of relationship with a man and I couldn't stand going through it again."

"You think I want to marry you for your house and family?" Marcus scraped back his chair and stood up, towering over her. "Of all the—" He broke off, raked one hand through his hair, then stared at her as if she'd lost her mind. "And what do you think I planned to do with you when I've tired of fixing up the ol' homestead and winning over the kids?"

Squirming beneath his irate stare, Lindsey bravely lifted her chin. "I'm sure you'd stick by me, but you'd probably start traveling more and more all the time so we wouldn't have to see each other so often. You'd be able to come and go as you please and we'd always be there waiting when you wanted to be with us again."

He swore under his breath and jammed his hands into the pockets of his pants. "For God's sake, why would I 'stick by you' as you so quaintly put it?"

"I . . . I know that you . . . desire me," she admitted miserably.

"Then why the hell am I offering marriage?"

"Because your moth—you're an honorable man, I know that." Lindsey recalled the conversation with Vera. "Marcus, I know that your mother would be terribly upset with you if she thought you'd hurt me."

"And it wouldn't hurt you if I married you for your house, kids and a good roll in the sack every six months? I thought I'd met most types of women, Lindsey, but you amaze me." It wasn't a compliment. Her mouth dropped open as he continued his tirade. "What kind of an idiot would marry a woman to get a ramshackle house in the sticks, two kids and a passle of demanding boarders? You wouldn't recognize the truth if it came up and hit you in the face."

His fist pounded the table inches from her cup, spilling coffee across the linen tablecloth. She jerked her chair away and stood up to avoid getting wet, but she would have been better off staying in her seat. Marcus stood right behind her, and she could feel his anger like a tangible thing swirling around her. She twirled around, saw the look on his face and began backing away as he approached. Finally, he backed her up against the kitchen wall and she was trapped. One of his arms was outstretched on either side of her head, his palms flat against the wall. He stared down into her pale face.

"When we get married," he reiterated each word fiercely, "I'm not leaving home until you get on your knees and beg. I'm going to totally ignore the children and be impardonably rude to your boarders while the whole damn house falls around our ears. I'll devote every second of the next hundred years to you, until you're convinced I'm marrying you for you and no other reason."

"But you don't love me," Lindsey reminded him, her eyes wide with astonishment. "You can't. . . . You never said . . ."

"Why do I kiss you, Lindy?" he asked, the anger appearing to have drained out of him after his furious harangue. Bending his head, he placed a tender kiss on the burning skin of her forehead. "Why do I cry when you cry? Why do I hurt when I think of you raising your children alone? Why do I want your boarders to like me, and why in hell do you think I care about that big old house?"

"But I thought you wanted to do the right thing. I thought . . ." She trailed off in confusion.

"Why?" He brought his body into sweet contact with hers, lifting her chin so she could read what was in his eyes.

She swallowed hard, hardly daring to believe it. "Because you . . ." He stood perfectly still, willing her to wade through her half-doubts and mishmash of jumbled thoughts. "You love me?"

It was much more a question than the answer he wanted, but he knew it would have to suffice until they could talk about it more calmly later on. He gave a brief affirming nod of his head, closed his eyes for a second, then gathered his courage to ask the only other question he had left.

"And you?" His hands fell away from her, his face a mixture of anxious tenderness. "I need the words."

"How is it possible?" Lindsey implored, extremely touched by his uncertainty. "How is it possible to love a man so much?"

"Lindsey." Her name was a warning, but his hands were gentle on her shoulders.

"I love you, Marcus," she said simply, and placed her head tenderly against his chest. "And that's why I kiss you. Why I hurt when I think of you going away. Why I cry when you cry."

"My darling angel," he groaned, lifting her off the ground and swinging her around and around. "I didn't think I could stand it another second."

Dizzy with happiness, she laughingly clung to him. "It's crazy, Marcus, but I do love you, I really do."

When they had expended their initial happiness and were once again reclining side by side in the conversation pit, she was secure enough to voice her fears. "I'm still afraid of some things. I see some big problems ahead of us. Peter was gone so much, didn't really seem to care about his own children, and they barely got to know him. I can't ask you to give up your job, yet I want the girls to know you. I'm not sure if I can handle such long separations."

He brushed a strand of hair away from her cheek

and slid his thumb over the outline of her mouth. "The twins will know me, angel. I took most of those overseas assignments because I was single. Most of my associates had families, but since I'll soon have a family myself, some other single man will have to take the long trips. I'll probably still have one long trip a year, but I fully intend to bring my wife and daughters along with me."

"Could we?" Lindsey's smile widened. "Really?"

"Yes, really," he mocked indulgently, then became serious as he saw she had several more questions to ask. Resigned to the forthcoming inquisition, he shook his head and made himself comfortable, cradling her in his arms as he lay back on the cushions.

Lindsey could barely think with her head resting upon his broad shoulder and his warm hand settled possessively over the curve of her hip. But she knew that it was time to erase all doubts so they wouldn't have to deal with them later on.

"Let's start with Peter." He encouraged her to confide in him, to trust him, and she did. She conveyed her anxiety about marrying again, describing her time with Peter and how he had always placed his job ahead of her and the children. She told him how Peter had made Althea feel unwanted in their home, and ended by conveying to him her fear of becoming too dependent on another person.

"I know you're not like Peter, but I'm not sure how much I've changed. It might be quite easy to let you take over everything and then I might end up as I did the last time.''

"Never," he exclaimed vehemently. "You are one of the most independent women I know. Look how well you've handled everything on your own. You hold down a job, support your children, cater to the special needs of your boarders and do it all without complaint. You've also done a hell of a job handling me. If I had had my way, we would have been married already.''

"Marcus!" Lindsey struggled up to a seated position, fending off his roving hands. "No one gets married that fast. We're going to have a proper engagement.''

"Proper?" He roguishly cocked a brow and raised up on one elbow, toying with the hem of her skirt. She gasped when he slid his hand beneath the material and began to stroke the sensitive skin behind her knees.

"How long do you intend to make me suffer?" His fingers began moving upwards, titillating the tops of her thighs as he edged himself closer. He ended up with his head resting in her lap staring balefully up at her.

"At least a month," Lindsey decided, rapidly losing her composure at his nearness. She lost it completely when he reached out and toppled her backwards, trapping her body underneath him.

"Two weeks then," she offered breathlessly, trying not to respond to the insistent pull of his kisses trailing warmly down her throat. "Oh!" she gasped when his fingers unbuttoned her blouse and began exploring the soft flesh beneath it. "Marcus, we have to think of the family." His lips started on the beckoning trail his fingers had left for him to follow. "It takes time to plan a wedding."

"My mother's a great little organizer," he declared outrageously, gliding his tongue over the hardened tips of her breasts. "We'll be fully occupied with other things."

"Marcus," she reproved sharply, but was too far gone to follow up on her admonition and much too eager to take an equal share in the "other things" he had mentioned.

Hours later, she smiled at him from her place beside him on the bed while he dialed the number of the house in Baldridge. "How can you think of calling your mother at a time like this?" She glanced pointedly down the length of his naked body, a blissful warmth rising in her cheeks as she recalled the pleasure she had derived from every inch of his smooth, hard flesh. "And like that."

Marcus grinned without the slightest embarrassment but tugged on the sheet until he had covered his lower body. "My mother won't know it's a time like this, and she can't see through the phone." His brow furrowed in a thoughtful frown, and a second later he slammed down the receiver and threw off the sheets. While Lindsey watched in open-mouthed astonishment, he got up from the bed, pulled on his pants and thrust his arms into the sleeves of his shirt.

"What are you doing?" she finally asked, trying

to decipher the cause of the slight pink tinge running under his tan.

"It just dawned on me," he said, buttoning up his shirt, "that my mother could very well know it's exactly a time like this and believe it or not, that's a bit unnerving."

Her shout of laughter brought a wry twist to his lips and a rueful glimmer to his eyes. She couldn't resist teasing him. "What a prim and proper man you've become. It makes me wonder about your outrageous behavior with me since we've met."

Giving an offended grunt, he stalked to the phone and dialed the number. "As man of the house, I'll have some respect from you, wench." He eyed her naked figure with an outrageous leer, making her flush. Without breaking the searing contact, holding her motionless with his heated gaze, he spoke loudly into the receiver. "Mom? Yes, well, Lindsey's decided to make an honest man of me." He laughed at her and sat down on the bed, then pulled Lindsey's reluctant, squirming figure into his arms. "It was the only ladylike thing she could do, since she's ruined my otherwise sterling reputation."

"I'll never forgive you for this, Marcus Stafford," she whispered and wrapped her arms around his waist, attempting to squeeze the hot air out of his lungs. He went on speaking with his mother totally ignoring her efforts to stop him. By the time he had finished with the conversation, she was resigned to her fate at his hands.

"I don't believe I'm doing this. Tomorrow? We're getting married tomorrow?" she mourned pitifully. "I'm dreaming the whole thing."

He gave the phone a dismissing tap and drew her down to the mattress. "All of our dreams will come true, angel." He lowered his head. "We'll enjoy one of them now, and tomorrow we'll begin another."

This offer expires March 31, 1994. Prices and terms subject to change.

YOU'LL BE SWEPT AWAY
WITH SILHOUETTE DESIRE

$1.75 each

1 ☐ CORPORATE AFFAIR
James

2 ☐ LOVE'S SILVER WEB
Monet

3 ☐ WISE FOLLY
Clay

4 ☐ KISS AND TELL
Carey

5 ☐ WHEN LAST WE LOVED
Baker

6 ☐ A FRENCHMAN'S KISS
Mallory

7 ☐ NOT EVEN FOR LOVE
St. Claire

8 ☐ MAKE NO PROMISES
Dee

9 ☐ MOMENT IN TIME
Simms

10 ☐ WHENEVER I LOVE YOU
Smith

$1.95 each

11 ☐ VELVET TOUCH
James

12 ☐ THE COWBOY AND THE
LADY   Palmer

13 ☐ COME BACK, MY LOVE
Wallace

14 ☐ BLANKET OF STARS
Valley

15 ☐ SWEET BONDAGE
Vernon

16 ☐ DREAM COME TRUE
Major

19 ☐ LOVER IN PURSUIT
James

20 ☐ KING OF DIAMONDS
Allison

21 ☐ LOVE IN THE CHINA SEA
Baker

22 ☐ BITTERSWEET IN BERN
Durant

23 ☐ CONSTANT STRANGER
Sunshine

24 ☐ SHARED MOMENTS
Baxter

25 ☐ RENAISSANCE MAN
James

26 ☐ SEPTEMBER MORNING
Palmer

27 ☐ ON WINGS OF NIGHT
Conrad

28 ☐ PASSIONATE JOURNEY
Lovan

29 ☐ ENCHANTED DESERT
Michelle

30 ☐ PAST FORGETTING
Lind

31 ☐ RECKLESS PASSION
James

32 ☐ YESTERDAY'S DREAMS
Clay

38 ☐ SWEET SERENITY
Douglass

39 ☐ SHADOW OF BETRAYAL
Monet

40 ☐ GENTLE CONQUEST
Mallory

41 ☐ SEDUCTION BY DESIGN
St. Claire

Silhouette Desire

42 ☐ ASK ME NO SECRETS
Stewart

43 ☐ A WILD, SWEET MAGIC
Simms

44 ☐ HEART OVER MIND West

45 ☐ EXPERIMENT IN LOVE Clay

46 ☐ HER GOLDEN EYES Chance

47 ☐ SILVER PROMISES Michelle

48 ☐ DREAM OF THE WEST
Powers

49 ☐ AFFAIR OF HONOR James

50 ☐ FRIENDS AND LOVERS
Palmer

51 ☐ SHADOW OF THE
MOUNTAIN Lind

52 ☐ EMBERS OF THE SUN
Morgan

53 ☐ WINTER LADY Joyce

54 ☐ IF EVER YOU NEED ME
Fulford

55 ☐ TO TAME THE HUNTER
James

56 ☐ FLIP SIDE OF YESTERDAY
Douglass

57 ☐ NO PLACE FOR A WOMAN
Michelle

58 ☐ ONE NIGHT'S DECEPTION
Mallory

59 ☐ TIME STANDS STILL
Powers

60 ☐ BETWEEN THE LINES
Dennis

61 ☐ ALL THE NIGHT LONG
Simms

62 ☐ PASSIONATE SILENCE
Monet

63 ☐ SHARE YOUR
TOMORROWS Dee

64 ☐ SONATINA
Milan

65 ☐ RECKLESS VENTURE
Allison

66 ☐ THE FIERCE GENTLENESS
Langtry

67 ☐ GAMEMASTER
James

68 ☐ SHADOW OF YESTERDAY
Browning

69 ☐ PASSION'S PORTRAIT
Carey

70 ☐ DINNER FOR TWO
Victor

71 ☐ MAN OF THE HOUSE
Joyce

72 ☐ NOBODY'S BABY
Hart

SILHOUETTE DESIRE, Department SD/6
1230 Avenue of the Americas
New York, NY 10020

Please send me the books I have checked above. I am enclosing $_____
(please add 50¢ to cover postage and handling. NYS and NYC residents please add
appropriate sales tax.) Send check or money order—no cash or C.O.D.'s please.
Allow six weeks for delivery.

NAME _____

ADDRESS _____

CITY _____ STATE/ZIP _____

Silhouette Desire

Coming Next Month

A Kiss Remembered by Erin St. Claire

Ten long years simply disappeared the moment Shelley Browning saw Grant Chapman again, but it was still a student/teacher relationship. Only this time Shelley wasn't concerned with breaking university rules.

Beyond Fantasy by Billie Douglass

Deanna Hunt had never known anything like the passion she had discovered with Mark. Hopelessly in love, she wondered if the architect who had shattered her perfect life would be there to pick up the pieces.

Chase The Clouds by Lindsay McKenna

Dany knew it was ludicrous to hope that a fiery stallion could ever compete as a Grand Prix jumper—but one look from the devastatingly handsome owner and all doubt was replaced by hope . . . to share in his impetuous dream.

Summer Thunder by Elizabeth Lowell

High fashion model Holly North had her work cut out for her: to prove to cynical rancher Lincoln McKenzie that her beauty was more than skin deep, and that her love was worthy of his trust.

Stormy Serenade by Suzanne Michelle

Top photographer Kiki Andrews had returned to Texas to photograph country singing sensation Stoney Blue—not to fall in love with him. But now that she had met the perfect man, she wouldn't allow him to escape.

Blueprint For Rapture by Lenora Barber

Enraged that he'd unwittingly hired a woman contractor, Phelan Cannon attacked Gabrielle at first sight with both anger and desire . . . awakening in her a hunger that only he could satisfy.